THE MATCH THROUGH HISTORY
FROM 300 B.C. TO OMG!

To Nancy!

Trust you get some laughs from this satire on the Eternal Quest for Companionship!

All my best —

Jeff Nelligan 9/21

P.S. Amazon Reviews welcome!

NelliganBooks.com

The Match Through History From 300 B.C. to OMG!

EPOCH AND *EPIC* DATING

By Jeff Nelligan, Ph.D, Faber College

ISBN: 9798517955661

Table of Contents

Dedication

To Jennifer, Ellie, Shannon, Sandy, Pamela, Patricia & Berni…for your inspiration. And "likes" 🖤🔥😂🏄💪👊❤️😎

Lighting a fire
with someone new. And old.

For centuries, Western scholars have puzzled over the private lives of the most prominent eligible singles in history. Endless volumes are filled with their monumental leadership, political, philosophical and literary accomplishments. But the really more complex yet basic question looms: *What about their dating habits?*

Whom did they seek and why? What were their most intimate desires? Were they hot or not? Perhaps most compelling, *what did they write in their online profiles?*

Now we know.

Relying upon extensive research into archival records found in New York, Paris, Prague, and Bakersfield as well as translating Phoenician hiero-glyphics and Instagram posts, our intrepid author reconstructs *quasi veritas* the dating app profiles of the most celebrated and socially needy bachelors and bachelorettes of the past 23 centuries. Revealed here for the first time ever is a timeless psychological panorama of longings – the soaring hopes and dreams, the nastiness and yes, "likes." Amongst the findings we learn:

- Forsaken to spinsterhood in Puritan Amherst, Emily Dickinson (screen name *EmmyD69*) longs for Mr. Right Now, not Mr. Right.

- Dylan Thomas boldly seeks "betrothal to a wolly-poppy American heiress!" and a lock on U.S. Citizenship.

- A dichotomized adolescence in the bad-boy corridors of Greenwich Country Day School leads Biggie Smalls *aka* The Notorious BIG to seek a Goldman Sachs equity partner with a "tight booty shizzle."

- Seeking to complement her INSP Myers-Briggs Type Indicator, Joan of Arc only will entertain "a major-league EFSJ with Socionics Te, natch."

- Henry David Thoreau (*Walden Hunkster*) desires a "smokin' lassie not afraid to get her petticoats dirty on my exquisite 14 acres of waterfront with its 40-foot dock."

- Mike Ditka has a defiant belief that "the 4/3 defense is the only way to a chick's heart."

- Caesar Chavez is "weary of stylized Latinx *mamasitas.*"

- "I am not a person. I am a collection of choices" maintains Virginia Woolf.

Previously wounded in love, lonely in life, defeated in the commercial battlefield space, angry victims of Tweet storms, London publishers, Russian emigre snobbery, Asian land grabs, Saudi businessmen and feckless peasant plagues and revolts, our match seekers persevere. Fundamentally, the profiles here go to the core of the historic courtship dilemma: Swipe left or swipe right?

Conversely, we also learn of the dark side - the emotional games, the filters, the posers and playas and bunny boilers: "I BLOCK all Romans!;" "Pray thee lassies, only daguerreotypes within the last five fortnights;" "No King Henry VIII supporters and their stupid MBGA hats!" "Contextualized Freudians can hang a louie!"

For our stalwarts the past is yesterday and tomorrow a scroll away. Opposites attract opposites attract opposites muses Kim Jong-un. Or as Charlotte Bronte says, "I will wait forever for thee. Just don't take too long."

"Meet Someone New" is not just a 21st Century trademark – it's a primal scream echoing across 23 centuries of dating apps. With this slender volume, we now glimpse anew the eternal human quest for companionship and how love is sought and found. It begins, as always, with a ♥

CHAPTER 1

In the Beginning…

300 B.C. to 1700 A.D.

Aristotle

Abstract: Born in 384 BC in Stagira, Greece. Diploma, Plato Tech; from *LinkedIn* profile: "Recognized leader in defining and promoting a thriving and positive construct of workforce philosophy. Successful in helping Enterprise and global brands navigate staffing solutions for creative, marketing, and *politos* hiring needs. Inspired and sincere believer in human brilliance; serious measurement expert, data liberator, policy disruptor, and promoter of authentic connection as the key to our individual and collective well-being. Member, Greek Senate representing 7th District, northeast Athens. Seeking synergies with like-minded partners to finance human services programs promoting high-end metaphysical solutions."

A GRECIAN CHURN / ATHENS

Viografia

The first thing you should know about me is that I'm a people person. That's what my Lyceum colleagues tell me and they should know -– we spend a lot of bro time together running the empire! I love watching people and then developing a complex synthesis of their various behaviors. I know - I can't help myself! But don't you think man is one of the most fascinating individuals on earth!?

If you agree, then guess what – we already share something in common! In fact, we are both witnesses to two cool people meeting each other! Get it?! That's the beauty of this app – it brings together people from the Mediterranean Sea all the way over to Persia, where the earth drops off!

Ok, a little about me: I do not botox, resurface, laser, get nails done, color my hair... what you see is all me... I have some wrinkles, non-flawless skin, several grey hairs... a couple days ago I walked into a Greco column near the Senate Lavatory ... yes, I actually did that and I got a concussion, and once the pain subsided was able to laugh about it. Life is too short to go without laughter every day, don't you think?

I more than dislike drama. If I see a situation as unworkable and have tried rationally to work things through, I just saunter away. And when I refer to drama, I'm not talking about life circumstances, I'm saying drug users, narcissists and Neo-Platonists - please move on from my page. Now.

I have a part time job as a Dad but I can make myself available whenever you are free. He attends college in Carthage and is super non-judgmental (like his old man) though he says he is getting a little tired of the city's Bright Lives Moloch (BLM) cult.

The people who know me best will tell you that I develop methods of inquiry that have exerted a unique influence on almost every form of knowledge in the West. But you know what Senators will say when they want your vote!

If my mind hasn't scared you off (I know! I can't help it!) let me assure you that the metaphysical game is just my day job even if it's hard work on the ole noodle.

When I'm not punching the clock as Senate Majority Leader, I like to "get my hobbies on." I do a little curating at the Corpus Aristotelicum and some freelance work for the *Athens Times*, mostly coverage of the Garden Club and 8-man football team over at the high school. I keep in shape with long walks near the Acropolis and I'm pretty good at Yahtzee.

Ok, pobody's nerfect - I do confess to some vices – like, some of my best treatises I owe to working the business end of some kush in a Grecian urn, if you know what I mean. Yeah, hookah style, baby. And if you can't handle that, then there are plenty of Macedonians on this app. Judge that ye not be judged – you'll read that someday, I assure you.

And yes, I've had a good life – finessed my way into Plato's posse, which gave me strect cred when I went out on my own. Then, check this out: I get a gig as a tutor for a kid who ends up conquering the world! You go Alexander! So I got that going for me, which is nice.

What I'm looking for? Well, since you ask Ms. Nosy Parker (just kidding!) I want someone who understands my love for metaphysics and likes angry, bitter arguments, someone with insight whose up for a little cheeching and is not all uptight about democratic norms.

And ok let's push the envelope here. Because I was born to be a teacher of young students and entire civilizations, here's a harmless little test: "For those who say that the universe is one something are bound to assert that coming-to-be is alteration."

If you want to get down with the G-dawg, send me a two-sentence interpretation of the above. The chickadee with the best one gets coffee and muffins at the Paneara two blocks over from the Parthenon! Go for it!!

Gallery

HAVING A FEW YUKS W/CONSTITUENTS

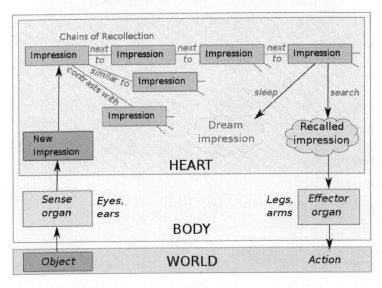

IF YOU UNDERSTAND THIS, YOU NEED TO CALL ME

DON'T ASK

Curriculum papyrus vitae

Widowed

Kids (1) and he doesn't live at home

Want kids? Why do you ask?

Religion: Aristotelianism

Drink: Who wants to know?

Job: Major league thinker

Education: More than you know

Athletic/fit: Delts to make you melt!

Smoke: Schwagmaster

Race: Sometimes

Exercise: Senate debates

Currently reading: *The Pelican Brief*

If loving this is wrong, then I don't want to be right

Curly fries with cheese

Things about me that surprise people

Consistently can pull off 20-plus stone-skips on the Aegean Sea

Weirdest gift I ever received

A plastic drachma!

Jeff P. Nelligan, Ph.D, Faber College

Cleopatra

<u>Abstract</u>: From *The Encyclopedia Britannica - Volume C, 2ⁿᵈ edition:* Cleopatra VII Philopator, born 69 BC in Egypt; Cairo Country Day School, Captain, Varsity Field Hockey. Career: Exotic dancer. Notable Contemporaries: Caesar, Antony, Pliny the Younger; Finalist, 51 B.C. Roman Senate Intrigue Sweepstakes. Currently: Conducting wars in eastern Mediterranean, gardening.

CARIO KAREN / EGYPT

If you think this site is nothing more than a place to "Pump You Up" Caesar-style, please consider before proceeding to fill up your papyrus with a bunch of phony hieroglyphs about how fast you ride a chariot and how big your Sphinx is, you grody nutjob. For Ra's sake, we're actual people on here w/real feelings. I speak for all my female subjects when I say we don't have the time or the heart to waste on someone with different goals. The last thing any of us need is some jerk at Club Med who tries to get jiggy on the ole cartouche. And no DRAMA – I have been through the *ba* and the *ca* of LTRs with a few Romans and I don't need it anymore. Those bastards bring nothing but heartache and drought and court shenanigans. ENOUGH! If you're a ROMAN, move along – there's nothing to see here!!

Ok, a little about me – I'll skip to the highlights. March of 51, BC - I had just been made Queen and my first act was a junket to Thebes to install a sacred Buchis bull worshiped as an intermediary for the god Montu. Yeah, tell me about it – little did I know it was the onslaught of the fried quail and mashed potatoes circuit. Things only got more crazy busy – a famine hit, flooding of the Nile south of Khartoum and then the bank calls and tells me the old man left me in major league debt - we're talking 17M Drachmas, which not even the IMF is gonna touch.

Anyways, your fixiecrat gets it chilled. Bull deal done, power solidified, paid down the debts with a bridge loan from BlackRock and a temporary (ha!) millionaires surtax and had the Corps of Engineers use some heavy duty hydraulics to get the Nile back on course. Bingo-bango-jing-a-jong-jango for the Cario K. Crusin' now.

What will you love about me?! I love to go out dancing – there's nothing like the groove of the sistrum and rattles overlaid by the melodies of a shepherd's pipe – you know, like early Yanni. However, I respect your space so dancing isn't mandatory for you.. ☺… SHOP – you best be at home in a bazaar because this loss prevention officer likes to get her shawl on at Tory Burch and Nordy's and guess what, where I go I don't have to pay.

Occasionally hit the gym – the Alexandria Planet Fitness hired Bikram – a totally odd and lovely man – for his signature hot yoga classes and there's a new craft ale bar next door. I will tell you that I'm a part-time singer in a dance band, which is my love… To find a man who sings, thinks he can sing, plays or picks ~lol~ an instrument would be great. But hell, even if you're tone deaf you're a lot better than the Roman chumps I got tied up with. Can I say there's nothing more romantic than listening to or playing music together? I'm the Queen so of course I can.

Ok, because we're being honest here, I warn you, I'm not close to my family. I had two of my brothers assassinated because they didn't get with the program. I really didn't know my parents, or that's what I tell people. But hey I simply LOVE LOVE LOVE all my nieces and nephews even if I can't remember their names. I visit them during the Thoth and Wag Festivals.

As for the down and dirty, during the week...I work...I've been with my current gig for about 17 years now, give or take a couple periods of exile. I like it enough...It pays the bills and I have full bennies, medical, dental, astrology. I should also add that I have never had a dinner partner who hasn't either fallen in love or wanted to be fast friends by dessert. Inasmuch as I have spent far too many years in the Rome/Athens cocktail party circuit, that is definitely not as impressive as one might imagine... Something unusual about me is that I've spent years and a small fortune on a painstaking restoration of a historic estate on the Phoenician waterfront near Tyre. Now that my children are grown I'm in the process of selling it and will relocate in the very near future. I know a lot of my married friends envy my single life but let me tell you, it gets old. Do I have to mention the ROMANS again?!?! ENOUGH ALREADY.

What am I after? My goal is to meet an honest, happy, smart, FUNNY, and "sexy to me" man. I want nothing more than to be in a committed relationship, with a man who makes me feel safe/SPECIAL. And who makes me chuckle every day. And don't tell me you're some kind of Caesar. I knew Caesar. And you're no Caesar.

HUMOR is so important, and I don't mean the eunuch kind – you know, the catty little whispers and innuendo. You like sunset/happy hour/quittin' time; Big Sur, Luxor, and Atlantis; sociology/psychology; day trips... you enjoy your career, but are not "addicted" to it. You are a good listener, but not extremely quiet. You are relatively ambitious, but laid back, low key, accepting. It goes without saying that you are genuinely kind and able to empathize with others -- I'm a Hufflepuff, what can I say?!

I would love to meet someone that is my equal, both intellectually and socio-economically. Distance is irrelevant to me if you are the right person. You will move to where I am.

Sigh … is this all too much to ask for? No. In fact, I'll take anyone as long as he's not ROMAN! Queenie Cleo has parted the kimono a bit here but trust me, I have even more to offer – get it?! Just send me a message via pigeon to NileHottie@pyramidinc.com Hope to hear from you before Rekehnedjes Days!

Gallery

ME AND CAESAR. MY FIGURE HASN'T CHANGED.

ANTONY LURKING - NEVER TRUSTED HIM

DINNER PARTY WITH THE BESTIES.

Just a tad more about me

Divorced

Kids: Yes, and they will never live at home

Religion: Ra

Drink: Dirty martini with blue cheese olives

Job: CEO, Egypt

Education: Yes

Athletic/fit: Just check out the Caesar pic

Smoke: Artisanal hookah

Race: Upper Nile

Exercise: Yoga, spin

Favorite Movie
Bridesmaids

Can't leave home without this
The 4th Ptolemaic Ranger Battalion

I know I've found the one when…
He doesn't perish immediately

Joan of Arc

Abstract: Excerpts from *Paris Vogue*: "…was born in Vosgas Province to dirt poor peasants. Early career: Religious visionary, corporate motivational speaker ("The Tony Robbins of Boulogne!") then seamlessly shifted into the armed conflict space and rapidly ascended from camp follower to Field Marshall. Demonstrated success during 11 months of the Hundred Years War winning battles of Orleans, Reims, and Castillion. Currently: Resolving legal issues involving cross-dressing and witchcraft.

INFP ENNEAGRAM TYPE 4 / ORLEANS

A propos de moi
Crazy busy military and Divine executive with wars in the northwest and constant tangles with royalty.

Born. Usual tomboy stuff growing up – plucking chickens, cleaning stalls, a little poaching when the boss man wasn't looking. Poppa and Momma felt my Myers Briggs vibe – they listened without judging or being exasperated by my often unusual thoughts, respected me enough and opened their minds to my new theories. And my visions.

Learned squat at Ecole - loved the theoretical and abstract but just loathed repetition of facts; didn't even take the SATs. Relied on my dominant function with a wee morsel of Introverted Intuition and insisted on following my own paths without any help from anyone else.

Advanced childhood – total full on INTJ adolescence, natch. Vision complex – had a strong focus on understanding the "big picture" of life. Even at 13 rocked bigtime on thought-provoking, existential questions. God, what can I do for you today?

How did it all come together for Joanie-O? Little bit of J (and I don't mean Jung) with a little bit of N - beginning at the age of about 14. I had a vision and no faux Luther deal. I mean, this was, like, real. You gotta understand the times. England wouldn't stop banging on us – our top marginal tax rate was at 85 percent and the so-called workplace protection rules on cobblers and blacksmiths had pushed us into a regulatory nightmare. Our leadership was as weak as granny's girdle and a bunch of Quislings, supposedly our countrymen, were in league with the British. The final blow came when the Burgundians raised a ton of soft money in a campaign to defund private militias. I'd had enough and perhaps the big guy upstairs had as well.

Here, we go flat out Jungian - two pairs of ng psychological functions: One was intuition and the other sensing. My instincts told me to hold back from the Janville trap and I sensed the need for full on offensive against the fortresses at Auxerre and Le Charite. Super Bowl wins and hey, if the troops want to get their loot on, that's their deal, baby.

Sometimes my perfectionism can overwhelm me. I do confess that I get irritated when my battlefield plans fail to live up to my vision; like, whose the wanker who gave me these outdated Ordnance terrain maps and will someone please get those damn wounded to stop their screaming! But I don't want anyone helping me – I can do it myself. For God's sake.

Sure, my therapist identified this as dichotomized ENTJ and ESTJ functions. Others asserted I was an ISFP in a Fi/Ni loop. I personally think

I'm really more driven by "vision" (N) and want things to instantly change through forcefulness (Ne/Te loop).

Enough of that psychobabble. Let's talk *moi.* My friends call me Joanie and yeah, if you've seen my profile pics, I do look a little young for my age. I was a cheerleader in middle school so you know I got a set of hot wheels. And let me tell you, you don't need SEAL training to learn how to lead men. Show a little leg on the Capri breeches, dole out the sisterly hugs, memorize some Providential exhortations and you can kick ass. And that's what we do.

What I'm looking for: You take your faith very seriously. In fact, with ole Joanie you can't take it seriously enough. You're part of the agrarian struggle and put your broad shoulders behind the right of national deter-mination. You're good with a lance but don't broadcast it. You like camp-ing, needlepoint, and close quarter battles fought in semi-arid climates.

Last, trust ole J-girl when she says that although two well-developed indi-viduals of any type can enjoy a healthy relationship, let's face it - INFP's natural partner is the ENTP or maybe even the ENFP. I need a guy that is dominated by Extraveted Intuition. I'm less concerned with the Socionics tab, roger that?

Long story short, I'm in a bit of a holding pattern right now, like I said, with some legal troubles having to do with silly witchcraft and get this – dressing like a man. I mean, c'mon, when are leather breeches and boots ever *de trope*?! I have a top notch public defender and he says Old Charlie who is otherwise a worthless sack of dung is behind me so I expect to be back in my hometown in a matter of weeks and ready to live the high life.

Now, when you reach out be warned that we get funky Wi-Fi sometimes here in the holding cells but keeping texting no matter what and I'll be in touch. I'm a persistent bitch. Just ask the British.

Gallery

ONE OF THE VISION DEALS

THIS IS MOI AT VERDUN

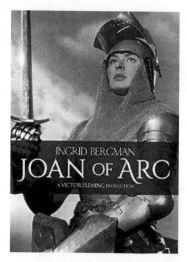

HOLLYWOOD DID A BIOPIC. WHATEV.

Instantane

Single

Never Married

No kids

Religion: All in

Drink: Water

Job: Field Marshall, Angel

Education: Not damn much

Athletic/fit: Fighting shape

Want kids? Yes!

Smoke: If ya got 'em!

Race: 10Ks

Exercise: Sieges

Can't leave home without this
Steel crossbow, breastplate armor, change of socks

Sons I like to sing in the shower
What's a shower?

Things about me that surprise people
Once hit a hole-in-one on a par four outside Reims

Joan of Arc responds to Mike Ditka's "Like"

Bonsior Iron Mike! *Merci* for the like!! I can see from your profile that *dur ou batard!* That pic of you in full battle gear is awesome ☺. But I didn't see a sword so I guess you keep that hidden (wink!) You can call me Joanie.

Joanie, nice to hear from you, doll face. Yeah, Iron Mike knows how to go to war for sure – ask Bill Belichek. That's some crazy stuff about the Jagueau Forest skirmish – what kind of defensive scheme were you up against?

Coach, gotta tell you - it was a freakin' cat fight! *Quelle*, I'm not on D much but when I am, particularly during hand-to-hand in a cramped village, I get my crossbowmen to hold the center and build on cavalry counterattacks on the flanks. What do you do for fun?

Good strategy – I bet the blitz works well with horses. For fun I mostly look at franchise opportunities, hit the dog races and Vegas. You? And does your cable package have Fox Sports?

We have a lot of foot races here in camp, as well as a blocking sled that we use for phalanxes – yeah, we get goofy during lulls (Smile). Oh, and my army controls a lot of sweet-ass vineyards in the northeast so we have plenty of wine and cheese meet-ups. I don't know what a Fox package is but I can already tell we have oodles in common – maybe we can take this offline for a phone call – my number is 867-5309. Hope to hear from you and keep on keepin' the D real!

CHAPTER 2

The Age of Reason.
And Ghosting.

1700 to 1800
Johann Sebastian Bach
Catherine the Great
Napoleon Bonaparte
Marie Antoinette

Johann Sebastian Bach

Abstract: Born 1685, Eisenach, Germany. Diploma, Hoch Conservatory, major: Harpsichord. From *Rolling Stone Archives*: "Career: Keyboardist for *Blitzkrieg*, a chart-topping heavy metal ensemble that won three Hoh's (Hohenzollern Platinum Single). Following the group's breakup, the "Duke" as he was known, bounced around with a chamber music cover band in Weimar. Saw Madonna's *Rebel Hearts Tour* in Berlin and reinvented himself as an EDM composer, turning out the *Brandenburg Concertos* and *Mass in B Minor*, earning himself two more Hoh's. Currently: Pushing the envelope on dubstep compositions in Bohemia with the *Graf Zeppelin Quintet*. Biggest Influence in his words: `Madonna, *naturlich!* My *uber fraulien!* Her shift from dance/pop to Synth has had a significant impact on my melodic flow, particularly her tracks on *I'm a Sinner*.' Fun Fact: Tunes his own xylophones."

ARCHDUKE OF POP / VIENNA

Uber alles mich

I see you on the street and you walk on by.

You make me wanna hang down my head and cry.

If you gave me half a chance, you'd see my desirer burning inside of me.

But you choose to go the other wayyyy.

I follow you around but you can't see, too wrapped up in yourself to notice.

Well, I've got something to say.

Don't try to run, I can keep up with you.

I've had to work much harder than this for something I want.

Don't try to resist me. Open your heart to me, baby.

I hold the lock and you hold the key.

Open your heart to me, darling. I'll give you love if you turn the key.

Gallery

MY ORGAN (WINK!)

SRO – MADONNA IN BERLIN!

SCRIBBLES AND DRIBBLES

ALBUM COVER, BLITZKRIEG'S *AVENGER*

Coda
Widowed

Kids: (19) Yes, some live at home
Religion: Lutheran
Drink: Fiji Water

Education: Weimar High -
the Fighting High-Notes!
Athletic/fit: Tip the scales!
Smoke: Cubans
Race: 1ˢᵗ Viennese School

Job: Composer, raver

Exercise: Conducting
Berlin Philharmonic

If loving this is wrong, then I don't want to be right
Tuba solo

Songs I like to sing in the shower
Papa Don't Preach

Who do you most look like
George Clooney

Things about me that surprise people
It's not a wig!

Catherine the Great

Abstract: From Reddit: "I was born Sophie Friederike Auguste, Prinzessin von Anhalt-Zerbst (what a crazy name, I know!!) Raised in Stettin, Kingdom of Prussia. I had a strict French governess (that chick was quick with a ruler on the knuckles during Latin verb conjugation). I excelled at home ec and swords and then climbed the notoriously fickle Russo-German aristocracy and came to power following a *coup d'état* that overthrew my husband (sorry hon, 'til death do us part – wink!) and second cousin (a total freakin' drip). Currently: Erecting (smile) Russian culture and arms to dominate the European landmass.

KREMLINKOUGAR / MOSCOW

I would soo date me!! Naturally kind, funny, positive, smart, a bit goofy, and pretty darn cute. Pride abounds for my annexation of the Crimea and the lands comprising present-day Poland and a decade's long career as a reigning monarch. I can always come up with a good solution. Get it? But, really I can. My favorite things include: Sports...Hounds, Billiards, Chess, the Moscow 49ers and the Lakers. Music...local Cossack bands in dive bars to icons like Ivan Manilow in large venues like the PetroDome. Food and Drink...Russian (of course!), Italian, Seafood, Mexican and chocolate anything. My love language is touch and I am awed by the power of words and the brute force of armored cavalry...the full moon sinking into the horizon, a brown bag of assorted Shiitake mushrooms ...

Listening to NPR while drinking morning tea (Minsk Blend with a splash of whole milk) - traveling!!! I've traveled a decent amount for my job signing treaties and I love it. After the admin jive is complete, I like sitting in a carpet gallery in Ankara playing backgammon and then touring the underground cities.

But I'm not some vacuous party chick. I have a serious side. I will say Earth's spin on axis feels extraordinarily wobbly these days and I toggle between hope and despair. I am courageous in self-reckoning and strive to pinpoint my complicity in the world's pain before pointing the finger at others. Something else unusual about me is that I've listed my actual age. Apparently that is rare, which I find perplexing... Finally, I've been widowed for the last two years. Ole Peter was a good guy, but so damn weak...sigh...

If you ask my besties, they'll tell you "Her Majesty has a masculine force of mind, obstinacy in adhering to a plan and intrepidity in the execution of it; she excels in the more manly virtues of deliberation, forbearance in prosperity and accuracy of judgment." Well, they should know!!

Sooooo, welcome to me and you! Be prepared to have the strength to love and be loved for the long haul, or short haul even. That's because I want to live longer not die longer – let's seek a meaningful connection and build a castle together. Or you can move into one of mine.

Gallery

TOLD YOU I WAS INTO HORSES!!

ONE OF MY SUMMER HOMES.

HOME OFFICE WHERE I CONDUCT MY AFFAIRS (WINK)

Vital signs
Widowed
Kids: Can't
Religion: Eastern Orthodox
Drink: Stoly
Job: Monarch. *The* Monarch.

Education: That hardass Governess
Athletic/fit: Curvy
Smoke: Gross!
Race: Aristocratic
Exercise: I'll tell you later

Currently reading: *Pies and Tarts* by Martha Stewart, anything Chekov

Most spontaneous thing I've done
Invaded Austria

Weirdest gifts I ever received
Diamond-encrusted contact lens case

The three things that make a relationship great
Pecs, biceps, abs, thighs

Napoleon

<u>Abstract</u>: Excerpts from recent *New York Times* profile:

- Born 1769, Corsica; Education Brienne-le-Château Military Academy; B.A., Siege Artillery;

- Kicked around Europe in various campaigns, known as 'The Tiny Steel Curtain' for expert pre-battle cannon emplacement. While in a bar on leave in Paris met and befriended Anthony Robespierre and the Jacobin Players;

- Sudden meteoric rise from 2nd lieutenant to Emperor of France from 1804 until 1814 and again in 1815, totally dominating European affairs;

- Current: Temporary hiatus to the island of Elba where he is planning his next European takeover.

NAPSTER / SOUTH ATLANTIC

Ma vie incroyable!

Who am I? Shameless self-promotion does not come easily to me. That being said and after *beaucoup* introspection about my outsize role in the world, here we go:

I am an intelligent, artistic, independent, risk-taking gentleman. A successful Field Marshal, part-time monarch and investor, I am tall, fit and I receive tremendous satisfaction working with my clients in maximizing high-performing real estate portfolios focused mostly on the Continent but with some side deals in Egypt and the North Med. Like they say in the 16th Arrondissement - *lieu, lieu, lieu.*

While this all sounds *je veux être tout droit, bébé,* I confess the details of my life are not for the faint of heart. I've lived and loved and laughed and have had my share of catastrophic failures, particularly in Russia. But I've persevered and find myself happily transitioned to figurative and literal exile on a marvelous island estate with 1.7 miles of Zone-1A waterfront and two deep-water docks. As we say in Elba: A setback is nothing but a set-up for a comeback.

Let's see...I enjoy cooking in a rustic though well-appointed field kitchen and I have yet to find a cuisine I don't like amongst all the nations I once conquered. I enjoy BBQ – *real BBQ* – and if you know what I mean, we have to talk.

Life can be difficult, especially in this madhouse called Europe, and I've learned to embrace the bad and the good and it has made me a better, much bigger man with many regrets and yet hope that something turns around. Adversity naturally brings a human instinct to offer comfort and advice, *n'cest pa?* Well, here's my advice: Don't march on Moscow if you're not prepared to spend the winter there.

I've always wanted a family – what I call I familia, but it didn't quite work out the right way and now I have a son who can't fill the old man's boots and two ingrates born above the sheets. One is a total slacker "managing" an artisanal pickle shoppe and the other fancies herself a performance artist. Nonetheless, I am proud to call myself a "grandfather" even though it's Grampy who's footing the jack for out-of-province tuition bills that are simply outrageous. I used to adore hanging out in Paris, Berlin, and rural Egypt near Luxor where I own a pear orchard.

What else? I'm left handed and dedicated to expanding my emotional availability to myself. And then there's the usual - classically overworked executive with too much time spent in airports. I know. It's all one helluva package – *quell dommage!!*

Who are you? I'll tell you. You love campfires and are at as home in the Louvre playfully selecting paintings you want hung in our country estate as you are in the forests of Bohemia living rough with a battalion of Lancers. There's a retro side of you that enjoys the folk songs of the '10s and yet you think Debussy is to die for. You're a real estate professional but your Jimmy Choo collection has sensible heels. Saturday night finds you at the discotheque and Sunday you are totally locked in with face paint and horns as a Paris St. Germaine fan.

You realize life is not just a collection of skirmishes with Austrian cavalry but a full-on campaign and you get along with the yeomanry much better than the typical countess. Perhaps you subscribe to the maxim that we only live once – trust me, with the Napster, it's twice or more. I won't promise you the moon but I have a fowling estate in north Saxony to die for.

Gallery

THIS IS HOW I EARNED THE BIG BUCKS

CHECKING OUT MY HOLDINGS IN EGYPT

RECALL WHAT I SAID ABOUT MOSCOW

Even more about me
Divorced. And Separated.
Kids (3) and they will never live at home
Want kids? Non!
Religion: Blood and Steel
Drink: Louis XIII Brut
Job: Mergers & Seizers

Education: Artillery
Athletic/fit: Tall and lean

Smoke: Only when stressed
Race: Corsican
Exercise: Forced marches

Things about me that surprise people
I'm really into supply chains

Song I'm embarrassed to say I like
Dancing Queen, ABBA

What's on your bucket list?
There's a two-mile stretch of unimproved waterfront north of Pas de
Calais that is absolutely screaming for development as mixed-use office
space and high-end condos with adjacent dining and shoppes.

Jeff P. Nelligan, Ph.D, Faber College

Marie Antoinette

<u>Abstract</u>: From "Desperate Monarchs" trailer: "Maria Antonia Josepha Johanna is no stranger to drama! Married at 14 to Louis-Auguste and known as the Dauphine of France, her one semester at Bennington in interior design paid off handsomely as she undertook a complete re-furbishment of the Palace of Versailles and the Seine Tower. It's been a hard-knocks marriage with Louie, simultaneously fighting off a nasty plague and feckless peasant revolt and cost overruns on the fitness center in the National Parliament. Favorite saying: `If it's not a Grand Palais, it's not an oven.'"

BABY CAKES / PARIS

Pauvre de moi...

Oh Love oh Life Oh Despair...My heart isn't into dating during this dark outbreak and these divisive times. Why, I hear that half of Brittany and most of Nice are just covered with peasant corpses. It's too awful to even think about / Hopeful the new *Département Français de la CDCé* will follow the science. Sometimes I wonder why I have this stupid app on my phone. Other times I don't. First impressions are important, a pic says 1000 words. You may be perfect for someone else. When I see that pic I'm just looking for me, not you. I'm spirited, honest, intelligent and well connected in the current court. I'm looking for a sparkle in your eye/ authentic smile! Your picture of energy and demeanor opens the door.

My mom says to date younger than me because she frowns on the eventuality that I'll end up taking my husband to the doctors or the morgue. Mom is right – what would we do without Moms? If ur one of the 74 million Charles II supporters with a stupid MFGA hat UR not my person. Don't write me to give me your thoughts - I won't engage and will block you. I am passionate about my political beliefs and am not complicit..... Confidence, CHARACTER, humor charisma in a man is attractive to me. I am Financially & Emotionally secure....You should be too. I am simple/sophisticated, elegant, direct, authentic and kind. Fave vacations: Bali, Napa, South Beach. Playboys not welcome - ur boring to me. If your second home is at a bar - we are not a match. My best match: intelligent, college educated, proud DAD with launched adult children, culturally Hindu or Jewish, tall 6 ft plus, fit, healthy, gorgeous smile especially when you look at me! Simple and deep - juxtaposition I see myself having a winter home/retired in 5 years. But open to other places, maybe the Hamptons. Mutual love for urban life, biking, yoga, live music & cafes, Netflix series, quiet time /reading, my loom.

You / No non- stop talkers – ur boring me. I know not writing back can be perceived as rude – don't worry – nothing personal. It's just that you don't measure up. I'm receiving way too many notes from people who fall outside my online criteria ur boring me. I feel no energy. Ur not meeting my expectations half way – mine too high and ur too weak. Be safe vs sorry during this awful plague – I hear Saville has been hard hit and they're running out of oxygen tanks. Too bad for them.

Gallery

ALL DRESSED UP AND NOWHERE TO...

I OFTEN BABYSIT MY NIECES

MEETING "REAL" FRANCE

Apres le deluge
Separated
Kids: Four, and they cower at home
Want kids? Not in this world
Religion: Will tell you later
Drink: Louis XIII Brut
Job: Interior design

Education: Will tell you later
Athletic/fit: *Mais oui*

Smoke: Yes, it's everywhere
Race: Will tell you later
Exercise: Will tell you later

Currently reading: Andrew Cuomo, *American Crisis: Leadership Lessons from the COVID-19 Pandemic*

I have always been strangely attracted to this
35-foot ceilings

Things about me that surprise people
My empathy

What's on your bucket list?
Getting to next month

Rihanna *"Hugs"* Johann Sebastian Bach

Well de mudda sick!! Peeped ur profile, Archdukz of Pop – wazy crazy!! OMG! U gotz to peeps mine, wahimbay. I beze 'de Black Madonna! And 'de Black Brahms! Me be from Barbados, mon, and I gotz the Austrian Beatz bigtime! U first or second Viennese School?

It makes no difference if you're black or white, if you're a boy or a girl. If the music's pumping it will give you new life.

You're a superstar, yes, that's what you are and you know it.

U great-kind-gubba to sez 'dat! And 'ya, jah bless. Me's have goodz run. In fact, Forbes Magazine recently calculated that I am the highest earning - per gross concert, endorsement, and album sales receipts - female singer ever, surpassing meze homegirl Mads. But I don't call dat George. Dat like buy ice and fry it. I beze a real homegirl. I knowz U dig what RiRi be trippin' 'cuz U be songmeister. Is that a wig or dreads – whatev – iz pistarckle! What be give U inspiration?

All you need is your own imagination. So use it, that what's it's for. Go inside for your finest inspiration. Your dreams will open the door.

Tru dat mon! Howz 'bout U get UR dreamy coco to the Signature Lounge at Munich and me G-650 be pickins' U up Thursday, 6 p.m.?

CHAPTER 3

"Thou goest to polka like it's 1899."

1800 to 1900
Henry David Thoreau
Emily Dickinson
Karl Marx
Virginia Woolf

Henry David Thoreau

Abstract: From *Brahmin Commonwealth Monthly*: "Born 1817, Boston. Education: Harvard College. Interned at family's pencil factory then took hiatus to "find oneself." Penned *Walden*, which critics dismissed as "a lazy, self-absorbed reflection upon life in a tramp's hovel which he later converted into a 6,000-square-foot lakefront retreat." His essay *Civil Disobedience* framed the 19th century Occupy Beacon Street movement. In his own words: 'I am deeply interested in the idea of survival in the face of hostile elements, historical change and natural decay and reversing it all through creative financing and value-added amenities.' Currently: Owner and manager, Walden Pond Estates."

WALDEN HUNKSTER / CONCORD

ewokmyweewok

Hola ladies, spanks for stoppin' to mac on the Hunkster. Roger your peepin' and backatcha big timey. Whazzup? You can call me Hank. Woodsy, laid back, creative, look good in a flannel smock and tan breeches, shy but not without a certain alphatude. And if you brought me home to meet your jefita she'd be treated to the finest squirrel stew she's ever tasted!

Right up front, cheggit - no games, no filters. The Hankster ain't a playa with a steelo – he goes by Commonwealth rules. It's gotta be all about honesty. Feel me?

If you ask my besties, here's what they'll say: "Good ole Hankums. Flippity flops in the woods getting' his wildlife on. Rocks over every Sabbath to mooch a dinch but his Platonist wit and easy smile makes up for wolfin' up three servings of sour mash pie. He sports a Roman nose but not roamin' eyes and why you don't have to worry about hiding the firewater, if you have any Hawthorne first editions be sure to secure them in the quilt trunk." That last bit is just an updog – the Hunksta no gleeper.

You get the picture. Ikeman - Jake Chillenthal, Hanka the lanka. Of course, the composite man would normally eschew such coarse generalities but this isn't BeanTownSingles.com

Jingling the change to say that your Hunkster isn't like the other abs on this site. You won't crack a j-ray on touched-up daguerreotypes of him posing next to a BMW (which are all probably leased anyway) or holding a four-pound catfish he claims to have caught in the Charles River or flashing a Schnappchat at a tavern surrounded by Patriot cheerleaders or in an outhouse mirror going all Hasselhoff. That's playa hokem.

I'm for real. Yeah, I went to Harvard and my family has made millions in the pencil and graphite game, la di frickin' da. The biggest dealio is that I live on 14 acres of exclusive waterfront in the best zip code west of Brookline. Beastie boy this - only 0.8 kilometers from the railroad station and 300 meters off the main road to Concordlandia. And oh yeah, a few of my essays have ignited a nascent Transcendentalism into a regional awakening. That be dope but no biggity - I find myself a didactic arbitrator between the wilderness in which I cower and the spreading mass of humanity in North America. Most certainly I decry endlessly the latter but I also feel that a teacher needs to be close to those who need the fauxskyn veritas, tru dat.

Now, in addition to trippin' wit' my soul, I'm also fanta with nature – the whisper of wood smoke on frigid New England mornings, herons skimming my private lake (did I mention the 40-foot-dock?) long tramps through the old-growth birch and a cozy cottage with 5G and the only Bose Wave SoundTouch IV east of Albany. I also have a well. And a spring. I think you'll find the spring charming.

And because I got the jack, I get the smack. So I beg thee to ignore the rumors, the backstabbers, the granny gossips and the village people. Jealousy reigns for my lakefront idyll, which did I note is surrounded by non-buildable-in-perpetuity National Forest?

I am seeking a Utopian pixie – outdoorsy and not afraid to get her petticoats dirty. I love canoeing, hiking, trail blazing, bird watching, fishing, fowling, falconeering and clearing brush on my 14 acres of heaven. I'm a vegan but pray that's not a deal breaker. I'm also totally ab-jacked because of the obstacle course I built on my estate – we're talkin' a costanza that utilizes the 120-foot oaks, the 80-degree inclines, boulder jumps, and the water obstacle swimnasium, all of which will make you sweat like a fat kid in sweet shoppe.

I'm also big time into innovation – why, I patented a graphite pencil that all the big dogs in Hartford and Springfield are trying to debo the kinfolk. But we won't even talk about that.

You may not be initially down with my austere, minimalist existence. That's skeen. Give it time. As my bmff Ralph Waldo says, opposites attract opposites attract opposites. Think about it.

We are all sojouners in this wide and vast horizon of existence. It's just that some of us sandoggies have made wiser real estate investment decisions. So think about mine. A weekend at my pad will blow your mind. Pinky promise.

Gallery

MY PEARL JAM PHASE

GUEST ROOM AT MY LODGE

GETTIN' MY HOBBY ON

JUST ONE OF THE MANY SWEEPING VIEWS
FROM MY WRAP-AROUND DECK

Single

Never Married

No kids

Religion: Emerson

Drink: Nada

Job: Graphite engineer

Education: Harvard. Next question?

Athletic/fit: Woodchopper's build

Want kids? Depends

Smoke: Bark (updog)

Race: Us

Exercise: My mind

Currently reading: Skateman Hawthorne

What I want to see most in the world
The movie *Caddyshack*

Things about me that surprise people
I can juggle five gourds at once

Weirdest gift I ever received
The foreman at my Dad's pencil factory gave me a three-sided parchment!

Emily Dickinson

Abstract: From *Amherst Beat!*: "This week's Lass-on-the-Go was born in in our charming village and educated at nearby Mt. Holyoke Female Seminary, where she majored in Latin and was Vice-President of the Enjambment Club. Following graduation she focused her career on writing unconventional verse and letters to "besties" all over the Tri-County area. Our Emmy has a penchant for white clothing, "mostly Dior and Dolce & Gabanna from the North Attleboro outlets" she tells us. She lives with Poppa on West Elm in a delightful old Victorian and laughingly calls herself a "serial vaccumer!" In her words: 'While most of my friendships have depended entirely upon correspondence, it's time to get my freak on!' Pray tell! These youngsters certainly live in a modern world and we know Emmy will have loads of opportunities ahead! You go girl!"

EMMYD69 / AMHERST

soml...

...thanks for stopping by! //it's like so weird to be on this app!! but BerkshireFarmer wasn't working out and i'll be dammed if i'm going on something called Tumble!! ok ok, emmy is a straight no chaser so let's get the jank out of the way up top... i really don't get out much and i still live at home...my old man has this big crib in amherst and while he's not exactly controlling i don't make too many moves without his permission FWIW.... but I don't tell him everything... a missie has got to have a life! – he'd probably bust his vest buttons if he knew i was out catting IRL so keep it on the down low if you see him down at the cobblers... /

????life in the mansion is not all bad…whatev – as one of the bronte babes said, i got three hots and a cot and my digs are an easy carriage ride to all of my besties… 😎 …that's another thing….my friends are very important to me..; the booges east on the pike in the big town call us pioneer valley girls…i mean..puhhhlease / GMAB!! i hang with this totally faboo crew….super smart, into embroidery and there's always someone around who is handy with a mandolin…but even with my dope amigos and a no-fuss no-muss home life there's something missing – i mean, like, it's great knowing all about assonance and iambic pentameter but after a fortnight or two that stuff gets old and i'm like so FOMO… i gotta live…baby emmy is not looking for mr. right, i'm looking for mr. right now 💚

Ok, a little about me//;: umm, soo, like, my faith is like really important to me – it's reformed calvinism in case you were wondering…/ -- with this great awakening jive going down these days the unitarians are all the rage and sometimes a girl has to get her straddle on donchaknow!!! ..so i do a little crossover dealio – … ease up on the predestination thingie while disavowing the trinity eschatology;; IK! OMG!! …the posse thinks it's sic but i say, like, this world is not the conclusion, a species stands beyond / invisible as music, but positive as sound…;/

..rog..as you can tell probably tell i do a little writing on the side… my poetry and a ton of letters to my biffles in nearby hamlets…and yeah, IMHO i think my stuff is danky but those grody bastards at Scribner's don't quite see it like stardust em…. i've also written a few folk songs about wondrous dawns around stockbridge and lenox… stuff which is totally derivative of rihanna 😕 … anyhoo, a few minstrels over in pittsfield promise me they're going to record a few of my tracks if they get studio time…

..////as for my poetry i'm mostly into natural phenomena – you know, sunrise and sunset, yaw… in terms of the imagery game, emmy's got it covered like auntie's funky quilt - religion, law, music, commerce, medicine, fashion, domestic activities and carriage rides that all probe, like, universal themes: the wonders of nature, power of mind over authority, the identity of the self, death and immortality, and shopping.. / / .. a couple dudes in the salon tell me the stuff is rich in complexity and subtlety of thought and carries a wagon load of metaphysical conceit... you know, the usual knitting bag of conjunctive motifs 😎 . but they're my peeps – what else are they going to say?!?

i try to get a few yuks in here and there, too, i mean, this century hasn't exactly been a freakin' laugh-in...there's this war going on right now which is awful and terrible and I just hope our brave boys in grey can stop those redcoats or Hessians or whatev before they get north of hartford. 😳

....three quick things you oughta know about me and if they're deal breakers, NBD and happy trolling to ya.

1.... i'm not into titling anything in case ole poppa goes peeping over my shoulder. ...the old man will then say i'm having the tumors again and the good lord knows i can't stand another stint in the village infirmary - it's hard enough making it to the outhouse here at the sugar shack - i know... TMI!!

2..... i'm consistent in my meter but i'm not some desperate slave to rhyming...// what i got working is the ole "slant rhyme"... YOLO!!!!

3....no punctuation, big boy – go non-declarative or even tachygraphy i always say. i like a bunch of ellipses and commas and googly gaws (i made that up!)..periodt....which was the grammatical style at my college, mount holyoke female seminary down the road. Old Maid City TBH... what a hoot.... i got enough demerits to fill a flour sack but i made it through.,,.. Trust ya process, as the ole parson sez......

...enough about my writing // what else? ..i have nine adorable cats who are ever so snickety and crickety in playing with my knitting....i mentioned the fun letters i write to my lit posse....oh yeah, my day job is being a seamstress but this sister has got a few gigs outside of the doily racket

JSYK.. one is taking care of the old house here, which really means making sure daddy has cigars and enough ale to float Old Ironsides 😊 i know i'm banging on the old man, but deep down, he's a good guy....or at least that's what he always tells us.

;;;...as for looks you can see in my daguerreotypes that i work out...no rolls for the e-babe....diet is like so croosh – i'm into herbs and roots and currently on a non-lard, non-rabbit diet;;;//....and if you're looking for my corset lines i already know you're a bad boy 😏 ...

....dislikes – please don't post any portraits of you in faraway places thinking that's gonna impress the Em / SMH // i'm after a man, not a gypsy... and let me lay it on the line - this chick isn't going anywhere anytime soon because i don't like to travel – long carriage rides make me positively ill and I find it impossible to hold a straight seam when the buckboard bounces around so...

likes - ....anything bronte....like i said, for early 19th century, those chicks can bring it in hot. 😎 ...also archery and needlepoint and churning 💚 !!

...i was in an LTR with a Judge here in town but he was older and his big thing was singing Methodist hymns – you know, "on a hill far away stood an old rugged cross, the emblem of suffering and shame" … i mean come on, dude, enough of the guilt trip...of course, not that i don't get a bang out of salvation / ; he was also married which after a decade clabbered my milk big time if you know what i mean...

...what am i looking for? ..easy – pretty much any man with a heartbeat who is near my age and not an old weezy like that damn Judge // .. oh, and not married/// i'm easy to get along with, just ask Oliver Wendell Holmes....i'm independent and don't need a muse, thank you.... i already have one and it's me… own your truth i always say .. the guy i'm looking for looks a little like Ralph Waldo Emerson who is totally baldwin and he's even come by a few times to sit in the parlor...but like i said up top / poppi is always hanging around and i never can seem to get Waldie in a compromising position if you know what i mean. 👀

....my guy has some shine on his saddle, que pasa? ...he gets a kick out of bobolinks and sylvan dells and waterfalls at midnight and he knows what i mean when i say "ere the eternal sky stretching towr'd Divine, mine arms sag helplessly as i try to hold up the sky" ...if you think that's bitchen then as the ole Negro spiritual goes, you be my number one homey.

...and don't fret - we have eight fireplaces in my Dad's home so you know i like to snuggle....i don't think i can relocate for love but you can try and convince me! ...besides, there's a nice boarding house a mile from Pappi's crib and i'm told they serve a good mutton stew....

....sooooo, if you like assonance and detest tagmemic grammar and can fill out the best parts of buckskin gherkin then maybe you're the guy for me! DM a telegram 📷 or better yet, drop me a red carnation along with a card and your room number at the boarding house... i can always get out if i tell Daddy i'm going to his fave vintners...don't wait too long – Waldo-boy is on the prowl and smokin' emmy has a feeling he won't be denied....

Photo Gallery

POPPA'S HOUSE — BORING

SELFIE W/WALT WHITMAN (YES)

MY FAVE FROCK (VERSACE)

opening the kimono (wink!)
Single
Never Married

No kids
Religion: Reformed Lutheran
Drink: Cider
Job: Writing letters

Education: yes
Athletic/fit: Tight, white
and out of sight ☺
Want kids? Hmm…
Smoke: Lassies don't
Race: Commonwealth
Exercise: 15 days a
fortnight!

Currently reading: emails

If loving this is wrong, then I don't want to be right
ellipses

Beach or mountains?
valleys

Things about me that surprise people
i can sew with one hand.

Karl Marx

<u>Abstract</u>: From the trailer to CNBC's *'Shark Tank'*: "Karl comes to us all the way from Prussia, where he received a doctorate in Industrial Psychology and a master's in Nihilism. He's the author of a so-called 'Manifesto' which he claims will restructure labor economics with an emphasis on profit sharing and increased social efficiency. 'Manifesto' was unsuccessfully shopped to investors in Paris and after his exile to the British Museum, Karl found no takers there either. Undaunted, he's now pitching in America. He told our producers he's looking for a handshake deal involving up to 49 percent equity in his theorem, which he says is a `priceless enhancement to capitalism.' Here's a fun fact about our contestant: He claims his last name is used as an adjective, a noun, and a school of social theory. Good for you, Karl. Now it's time to man up with the big boys in the toughest shareholder meeting on the planet – Shark Tank!"

THE DIALECTIC! / LONDON

Mich!

The people who know me best say that that I go overboard on life because I want to fundamentally change society. But who asked my Mom and Dad?!

Welcome to my profile and thanks for giving me the ole *gib mir den Blick heiße*! If you're like me, *liebchen*, you always see things in a half-full tankard kind of way - and what you don't like you work to turn upside down until it's to your liking. That's because the Dialetic is not a game, *wunderschön*, it's the new frontier. *Ost front uberalles!!*

I think life should be lived day by day, not the other way around. Sure, I play the loose *lustiger* at times but I'm known for some coarse *lumpen* humor. Btw, there's so much to learn from the dawn of the industrial age, *ein?!*

Seufzer ja, I've won, I've lost, I've laughed, I've watched pitched street battles from a safe distance. But enough about ole Karlie, as my close friends call me (and Mom and Dad ☺).

What I must absolutely have…

You should be an Enlightened women. You're as comfortable in a kitchen making great pots of stew for the organizing meetings as you are in full revo-mode distributing leaflets at a riot. You are passionate about editing circulars and you are savvy in the New Stenography. You see yourself on the frontlines of social justice and should have no less than 2K followers on Instagram.

In addition your proletarian ardor you like your quiet time. You adore Bartok and Wagner (even though he's a Bismarckian tool) and your fave sport is fowling. Nothing pleases you more than long walks on the moors (even though I'm Prussian I've spent a lot of time in Britain – passport troubles, you know) and looking for deals in the charming little antique shoppes on the outskirts of Birmingham. The overthrow burns within you as we snuggle by the fire and plan our takeover.

Ein?! So if you like what you see send me a telegram! And please, if I reach out, don't ghost me. Our revolution is all about honesty. Or else.

Gallery

THE GOOD OLE DAYS IN PRUSSIA

ONE OF MY BOBBIES (#HUMBLEBRAG!)

BFF – THE FREDSTER ENGELS

Hier ist noch mehr!
Widower
Kids: Yes, and they live in exile
Religion: Leninism
Drink: Peoples' brew
Job: Philosopher, gaddabout

Education: *Veil*!
Athletic/fit: Scholars build
Smoke: Ein!
Race: Upper Silesia
Exercise: *Ja mein* Bowflex

Zombie attack...run, fight or join them?
None of the above. Convert them.

What is your favorite tool?
Toro Power Curve 18 inch OHV 4-cycle snowblower

Fave place to hang out
Reading Room, British Museum

Virginia Woolf

<u>Abstract</u>: From an excerpt of *Sisterhood Chronicles - Where is She Now?*: "Ms. Woolf was born to womyn in 1882, christened Adeline Virginia in South Kensington and took her education at the Ladies Department, Kings College, London. A major in cross-stitching promised a bright career but a recession in the loom industry prompted her pivot to success as a modernist 20th Century writer who pioneered the use of stream of consciousness as a narrative device. The weaving game's loss was our gain! Currently, Ms. Woolf is dealing with some pesky health issues but with a Peloton subscription is now on her way to a new start! We wish her the best!"

IGINNIETHEEME? / WORTHINGHAMSHIRE

What is the use...
Why, pray tell, is this called an essay? If I want to show you how I arrived at this opinion about the room and the money, don't tell me it's an essay. It's *me* - I'm showing you about me – her metaphysical gewgaws and a river of twine which funnels into no structures or strictures or sutures and satraps. Satraps are Pakistani blacksmiths. Let us get down on it.

I am not a person. I am a collection of choices. I smile not often and my wit is infectious when I'm singing hymns from a lonely church pew.

Anglican. I live near the millrace right down from the granary. Benjamin Franklin once said – and Leonard told me this – that a person wrapped up in himself makes a very small bundle. You should never be that person and neither shall I because my body is my canvas. In my life there are always rustic burlap wedding invitations to sort through and whimsical window shades hiding the glory of tiered macaroons.

I am awed by the power of words. That's why I use them when I'm speaking to you. We all live in a house of language where words come together like distressed oak crossbeams. Words can also take up space in the time continuum, like when you're taking to someone in line at Harrod's. There is no end to the words you can use. Or say.

My friends describe me as "real" not "fake." But again, it's not about me. You have an uplifting personality and glow and have been separated longer than three hours. You listen to the BBC while drinking absinthe and you've seen every episode of *Inspector Morse* four times. What do you like? I'll tell you – you like a clipchin of assorted butternut squash from the Soho farmers market on alternating Tuesday's. You are funny without being humorous. You quote from Trollope but only when it's unnecessary.

I don't believe in the use of exclamation points in profiles so if you do then please stop. Your type doesn't interest me punctuation wise. Also, I like Karaoke, deep sea fishing, and collecting 18th Century hurricanes. But living alone for two years has given me a profound appreciation for company. The Second Law of Thermodynamics is theory and practice are only separated by time. What is the First Law? I will tell you. Heat is a form of energy and subject to something I can't remember. Better now?

I've invented my own language. It's used in a reality fantasy screenplay deconstructing this app, an electronic cotillion beneath the chandeliers of which floats a feeble and heartwarming attempt to find an answer where there is no question. Long live the Queen. Joy is my default except when it isn't. I like swing-dancing, heraldry, taxidermy. Oscar Wilde one told me that if you are not too long, I will wait for you all my life.

I see you – smiling, laughing, and sharing all our interests. I see you seeing me in seeing you. My friends describe me as "real." That wretched Bloomsbury crew just shrugs. Did you ever try to catch a rainbow? I think the most important thing about a person is their passion for something in life. Do you ever get bothered by the overuse of certain words? Like passion?

I don't use the letters X or x. I see you – smiling, laughing, and sharing all my interests. I see you seeing me in seeing you seeing me. Excelsior.

Gallery

WHERE I HAVE A ROOM.

ME AND A VERY CLOSE MALE FRIEND. MY DEAD HUSBAND.

DID I TELL YOU I AM INTO BOOKBINDING? NO.

ohhhhh…

Single	Education: Why…
Widowed	Athletic/fit: Who cares?
No kids	Want kids? Too weak…
Religion: Anglican. And Mahomet.	Smoke: Weak…
Drink: When I'm thirsty	Race: Against time
Job: Ballerina	Exercise: I mean, really weak….

If loving this is wrong, then I don't want to be right
Charlie Chaplan's tuna casserole.

Things about me that surprise people
Absolutely nothing and everything.

Weirdest gift I ever received
A room of my own.

Top three things on my bucket list
Satraps?

Caesar Chavez "Turbo Winks" Emily Dickinson

Hola hottie! Loved your profile and who says you don't have some *bueno* corset lines?! *Aiiii!!* CC also go *loco* on your prose style! It has a verve and pace that is so intriguing – guessing your influences are Wharton and the Bronte's, si? And I totally agree with you – grammar is nasty! Are you enjoying this incredible spring weather?

....oh cc rider man...what a charming note...,...you're a dear heart for reaching out ....i don't have the chance to meet any spanish peoples... in fact you're the first one...so hola bacakatcha ☺...you are soooooo perceptive...yes, edith and the b sisters and also george eliot, who is a total fave &?? // .goodness gracious, from your profile you do indeed sound like a very crazy busy man...fighting for the civil rights of down trodden workers... so that's where tomatoes come from!!!!...i've had two and both were delish///... for fun i go to quilting bees and workout with the berkshire county line dancers association...we put on some fab shows with ukuleles...and yes i've heard of mexico – wasn't there a war there a couple weeks ago...and i must ask...what is a chiquita – i've always wanted to know!

….my dearest rider boy…i haven's received a telegram from you in sooooo long…maybe you're on one of those picket lines at a port of call or taking it all offline at that orchard in san bernardino you told me about…i was so uplifted with your description that i started a poem ///….a drop fell on the apple tree …another - on the Roof…but I can't find a word to rhyme with tree!!!!! …i hope you are doing wonderfully and not taking the coward's way out…you didn't promise me anything but that doesn't mean you don't love me….ralph waldo is back haunting the drawing room with poppa…so if I don't hear from you soon…sigh…as we say in amherst, it'll have to be asta lavaista baby…

CHAPTER 4

From Breakfast at Tiffany's to It's Just Lunch

1900 to 2000
Dylan Thomas
Eleanor Roosevelt
Margaret Thatcher
Ayn Rand
Caesar Chavez

Dylan Thomas

Abstract: Excerpts from *The Welsh Academy Encyclopaedia of Wales*: "*Cymraeg i Blant yn* Swansea *cynnig pob math o weithgareddau hwyliog i* Herald *blant a'u teuluoedd,* whisky *gan gynnwys sesiynau tylino babi a ioga babi, a grwpiau stori a chân* wireless *Mae gwybodaeth am y chefnogaeth bellach i* Glúingel, Bodhmall, Cathbad, Gwench? *dy ar llyw.cymru i hlancymraegiblant neu* U.S. Passport *chwilia am Cymrae."* (English translation: "Our beloved kinsman was born in Swansea and worked as a Herald reporter where he was fired for drinking on the job. A pilly-pally mystic muse of fairies and sprites, he pursued radio broadcasting and earned a reputation for catchy lines: "Do not go gentle into that good night" and "And death shall have no dominion." Fun fact: Named his three or four children, Glúingel, Bodhmall, Cathbad, Gwench? after Welsh druids. Currently: In Wales looking for a way out."

Jeff P. Nelligan, Ph.D, Faber College

DYLLYDEE! / SWANSEA

All About Mee-kins!
A billow-cheeked hi-dee-ho and a candle to 'ye altar wise by owlight in the halfway house! More: A dandylicious randy slocum to the lovely lasses who stumble backwardsly forward onto this rosehip jolly-wolly portraiture of a soul who joyfully hobble-de-gobbles the bursting bloom of an O'Keefian black iris. If you know what I mean. I'm Dylly and silly and methinks and meknows I live in a magical world where illusion and allusion are crammed together like gutternsnipe laundry in an alleyway catty-cosy corner to the jumble-tee wicket!

Mee-kins? Verse is my day job and while it pays the bar tab, I'm looking for an LTR that brings me to the mansions of glory set in the moss of a Celtic kitty-winkums kitty-corner to a fantasia of mystical cherubims with fancy dainties at moonrise!

I'm easy to tolerate but hard to understand. Me's spirit goes forth beneath your moon, oh sensuality, crying like a cat. Only the wiser amongst you Flowers will realize I lifted that gem from a Yankee woman and if you can tell me whom, you win a ride in my chariot of gossamer pulled by multicolored unicorns with the map of the starworlds tattooed on their foreheads! Eeee!

64

It wasn't always like this for DylliestDee. Before the odd linguistic dealio kwitched, I spent time in a hardscrabble stony place between the Walesian warp and woof of grinding poverty and wayyyy too much of the brewer's barrel. I was a slack-jawed johnny but ye knows a druid named Jameison Stout urged me to flee the centurion stalls and the nani-nani Momsie and Popsie world. With only a tabolly and a quill I've managed to eke out a sip and simmer living with candied lines and a prose style that is simply marvilicious.

I sallied forth to the great good America and delivered well-received lectures at high institutes of learning as well as poetry slams where the Dionysian spirits everflowed and the honorariums were mollykins. Alas, there ensued a forced return to the merry land of wee because of a critical class weary of my sheeny shenanagins.

Hear me o' lillylasses! Me wants to tumbly humbly back on bobolinks to the leprechaun forests in Manhattan or the Hamptons and get U.S. citizenship through the merry betrothal of a pixie wixie with starshine in her eyes and a goldmine in her pockets...or her Poppies pockets!

I dare you to capture the quicksilver with me, those tilly-billy streams that run through our hands in a silky platinum plinny as we burst the moon-shadows with my Cockeny cantor and your dappled doubloons. Passport is current and damn well set on getting the hell out of Wales and hoppily happily relocating for love!

Gallery

No, I wasn't drinking!

My office in New York.

Where the hell is that waiter
with my Perrier?!

Peekaboo!
Separated

Education: Swansea
Elementary

Kids: 3/4 – wee bens, some-see-wheres

Athletic/fit: (ok, writer's
paunchio!)

Want kids? If you do, beedly bee!
Religion: Tuatha Dé Dananns
Drink: Occasionally never
Job: Teller of tittle-tattle

Smoke: Only when awake
Race: Druid
Exercise: My right arm
(wink!)

For fun I like to
Talk normal

Things people don't know about me
I once threw a phone book at Bertrand Russell

Beach or mountains?
And green and golden I was huntsman and herdsman, the calves
Sang to my horn, the foxes on the hills barked clear and cold,
     And the sabbath rang slowly
   In the pebbles of the holy streams.
So, mountains.

Eleanor Roosevelt

<u>Abstract</u>: Excerpts from *Town & Country: The Roosevelt Edition:* Parents: Both Roosevelts. Education: Allenswood Roosevelt Boarding Academy in London, Major: Phys Ed. Career: Married at 21 to fifth cousin, Theodore Roosevelt, who would become infamous as a Depression-era, wartime and misogynistic U.S. President. Upon his death, Ms. Roosevelt founded Another Roosevelt Foundation and reinvented herself as global civic and educational patron. Currently: United Nations Special Ambassador seeking a witless bohunk.

HYDE PARK PUMA / NEW YORK

Why hello there!!

Once when I was a very young girl horseback riding with my great-uncle on our family estate, he said, "Elly dear, here's a little piece of advice from your dear old Uncle Teddy-Wampums: Stay away from the chicken and mashed potatoes circuit." He was a delightful old codger and President at the time and being brilliant for my age, I instantly knew what he meant – don't ever marry a politician. Good God, if I had only listened to him I wouldn't be on this appalling app looking for a non-family member to date.

Here's my truth, hombres. My whole life has been a drawing room lie; I've been a victim of stifling boredom and misogyny and deceit. Dearest

Wampy-Wamps was right! You make the mistake of marrying a fifth-cousin who is a politician and suddenly he's the Big Man and you become the Little Woman – the faithful wife, the preening companion, always the one pushed in front of the radio microphones and the WPA ribbon-cutting events and War Bond Drives and the newspaper reporters. Always the loyal sycophant who represents the Big Man with charm and intellect. The one who is the last to know the Big Man is getting his infamy on with a harem of New Deal dollies.

Oh, but it gets better. One day, the Big Man gets sick even though I told him not to go swimming that time. Suddenly he's complaining about his stupid back and his scraggly old legs hurt and he's getting massages all the time. Total, utter hypochondriac. But oh, that doesn't stop him from smoking like a chimney. And soon the Big Man is Wheelchair Man and then Dead Man, floating around lifeless in a hot tub in Georgia in the midst of dictating correspondence to his mistress. I'M SO DONE!!!

Enough Big Men, enough power brokers with their schemes, enough Senators and Governors and Wall Street barons putting the moves on, enough Society List pretty boys and Ivy Leaguers and their cigarette holders and monocles and Long Island lockjaw. Craven bastards. I'll tell you what, boys. I'm looking for a simpleton – a brawny roustabout – a brainless hunk.

And here YOU ALL ARE on this ridiculous site. BIG, powerful men – pipefitters, maybe - holding up fish you've caught, standing proudly next to your shiny, powerful roadsters, yukking it up with your broad-shouldered mates at taverns while downing hard whiskey, your massive forearms and granite jaws and close cropped hairlines just above your eyes, unkempt and unshaven and quite frankly unbelievable in your manhood. REAL MEN!! Men who live hard in stained clothing and hobnailed boots and greasy kerchiefs – the true fruit and iron of America - auto mechanics and plumbers and railwaymen and farmers and herders and rustlers. Hell, none of you have even seen a wheelchair and the only estate riding you'll do is on a tractor near the servants' quarters. Oh, I know YOU – you're a factory worker – and I only ask you to fulfill me, this shy, cultured doyenne of high society. I need only one of you. Or maybe two.

I'm widowed if you haven't guessed by now, you magnificent, slow-witted stud. Good Lord, that deceitful bastard and his fotties in Yalta and Hyde Park and the West Wing and the War Building. Am I going on too much about him? I CAN AND I WILL. I'm SO DONE!!

Here's the dealio - I'm looking for my future partner, playmate, lover, and best friend – did I mention a coal miner, perhaps? Someone to feel safe and secure with, someone to lead me in a sensual, loving relationship. Or just SENSUAL. Do I have your attention? Let's get to know each other. To know me is to know that I am kind, affectionate, active, easy-going, warm, adventurous, playful, passionate, athletic, outgoing, supportive, and well…a Roosevelt.

My idea of a relationship going forward is one where we can stand each other with no drama. You are – you're a longshoreman, *n'cest pa?* – and you're TOTALLY FIT and rocking six-pack abs and even if you're dumb as dirt, I know we will have NO DRAMA. We can be like those older couples on tv commercials going from one adventure to another in a Subaru… only I'm 30 years older than you and it will be a Rolls.

You're someone I look forward to seeing, someone who loves to laugh even if it is your affinity for Three Stooges re-runs. You should know that I like the predictability of a daily routine – a charity appearance in the morning, a couple of media interviews, paperwork and admin time in the mid-day, an early cocktail party and then we hit my pad on Park Avenue and relax and light a fire… and I will only consider myself settled when that FIRE is lit INSIDE ME.

Life is too short, don't I know, to be without desire or passion…if I message you, there is an attraction based solely on your photos – you're a steelworker, yes - and don't even worry about the misspellings in your profile.

A lot of people call me "one of the most esteemed women in the world" but that doesn't mean jack if I can't have Jack or John or Jim - a pipefitter? - a real man as opposed to the worthless husk I married. Now take a trip with Elly – I'll pay for everything.

Gallery

ONE OF MY PORTRAIT SITTINGS

MAYBE A SOLDIER?

THAT'S HIM, THE BASTARD

ONE OF MY BESTIES

Bring it on

Widowed

Kids – 6 and they have their own estates

Religion: Episcopalian – Highest

Drink: 1910 Rigonier

Job: Ball-breaking non-profit fundraiser

Education: The best

Athletic/fit: Big frame, don't fill it

Smoke: Only when around Churchill

Race: Goodness gracious!

Exercise: Jane Fonda's Workout

Currently reading: My speech to the United Nations

I got in the most trouble for…

Banging on Truman in October of 1948

Weirdest gift I ever received

A bauxite mine, on a mission trip to the Belgian Congo

What's on your bucket list?

Get my freak on in Warm Springs

Ayn Rand

Abstract: From Harper-Collins Publishers website: "Born Alisa Zinovyevna Rosenbaum, Aynnie draws from her life story when writing about the experience of a young, jilted Russian aristocrat turned philosopher and chain smoker. Exiled from St. Petersburg, she came to the U.S. with dreams of becoming a life coach. Stymied by the Tony Robbins' *junta* she turned to writing, producing two best-selling novels, *The Fountainhead* and *Atlas Shrugged*, which have ignited a world-wide firestorm featuring Objectivism, a philosophy loosely based on Projectivism. Currently: Working on a sitcom featuring the hijinx of a Russian family-owned restaurant in Denver that refuses to serve Balkan emigres.

StPetersbabe / New York

A Note to Readers

The author endeavors to establish some preliminary parameters to govern the journey you are about to embark upon and thus requests you clear your mind of ontological materialism and instead seek an equilibrium consonant with our Objective compatibility. Of monumental importance is the concept of man as a heroic being with his own happiness as the moral purpose of his life. Productive achievement is his noblest activity; his reason as his only Absolute. To deal with men by force is as impractical as to deal with nature by persuasion. If this does not resonate, please close out this profile and move on to the next one.

Jeff P. Nelligan, Ph.D, Faber College

Our first step...

Imagine a dystopian United States in which the most creative industrialists, scientists and artists respond to *blagosostoyaniya* (welfare statism) by going on strike and retreating to a mountainous hideaway where they build an independent and free economy. Imagine one man, an average archetypical hero, who leads this strike. Surrendering to the wretched informality of this age we'll call him Johnny - who in his understated and eloquent fashion describes the strike as "stopping the motor of the world" by withdrawing the minds of the individuals most contributing to the nation's wealth and achievement. Imagine this strike illustrates that without the efforts of the rational and productive, the economy would collapse and society would fall apart. Further imagine that this haunting tale includes elements of mystery, romance, and science fiction and contains a compelling but too-short monologue on a breathtaking new philosophy sweeping the best salons of Paris, London and New York. But not Moscow.

If this does not resonate, please close out this profile and move on to the next one.

However, if all this makes perfect sense, then you have permission to read the rest of this extraordinary tale.

The authoress is from the Old Country and here is Test #1: If you are unaware of where that is, then you should please close out this profile and move on to the next one. Test #2: If you passed #1, note that this person's childhood was spent in a quaint little burg built on a swamp that just happened to be named after the greatest military and diplomatic genius to stride the world. What is this city's name? Time is almost up. Aha, maybe one, two fortunate suitors remain.

Enough of the author's worldview but not her exquisite need to toggle between the second and third person narrative. You know her. Or perhaps

74

you don't. As for her childhood, she grew up good times and then very bad times. When the Czars ruled, the rivers ran with wine and the sky was blue all the way south to the Pripet marshes. And then. Then, a cold wind blew, followed by a black armored train from the southwest, Leipzig to be exact. Her patriarch lost his job at the Court, the family sent fleeing to the Crimea with only nine trunks apiece per family member and a new oligarchy, disguised as the worthless proletariat, suddenly controlled the levers of government, forcing your poster girl here to board a modern steamship bound for the New World.

Oh, *stanovitsya luchshe*, it gets even better. Hardly welcomed as an A-list émigré like Melania, our correspondent has very limited commercial success. She's blacklisted by the Marxist literary industrial complex of that day (indeed, your author notes that horrid man is on this platform – a bearded, swarthy bastard going on about collectives. Ladies, I know you cannot read this but don't go anywhere near him. He'll break your nation. Please close out his profile and move on to the next one.)

Our champion didn't falter (she never does). She kept grinding - a tall, winsome woman in dark power tweeds, sensible shoes and an eccentric flair for smoking tiny cigars in a Czar-era cigarette holder. She dabbled in non-fiction but found the art form so constraining. Brute facts are for brutes, she would always say, and it's infinitely wiser to soar with the imagination and make everything up. She's certain you'd agree.

Recall that that soaring imagination referenced just now? That was mine and it was my modest effort in turning the Western philosophical canon on its head. The MSM panned my masterpieces, oh yes, but my genius ignited the worldview of a silent majority of thinkers, writers, and even peasants. If you're fortunate I may provide that worldview on our first Zoom.

And now I'm throwing the long ball here when I tell you I adore romantic realism. Because that is why, dear boy, I'm on this wretched site.

All coming together for you, *babushka?* I see you nodding your head and agreeing with your frisky FountainGirl that the West has nothing to offer us in terms of philosophers. If this does not resonate, please close out this profile and move on to the next one.

Enough about my historic, global intellectual achievements. What am I looking for?

More than what I find in best salons – only sycophants there and others who don't agree with me. I want a *goryachiy paren'* and if you have to look it up then I won't repeat myself. You know what to do.

If there's even one man with a pair who is still with the St. Pete Babe, then perhaps you come close to but do not outpace my considerable gifts. An LTR would be nice but don't let that hang you up. Our souls – non-Divine I must emphasize – are not into time. I've had mixed reviews all my life but what do the critics know? I believe in morals alright, the morality of rational self-interest. If this is ringing your gong, then ring mine.

Gallery

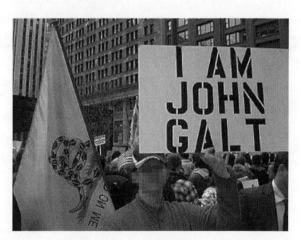

ALL PR IS GOOD PR

57ᵀᴴ EDITION. WORD.

SMOKE 'EM IF YOU GOT 'EM!

Brute facts

Single	Education: More than you'll ever know
Widow	Athletic/fit: Vogue Girl, 1924
No kids (thank God)	Want kids? Not for this world
Religion: Not	Smoke: Anything that ignites
Drink: Acqua di Cristallo	
Tributo a Modigliani	Race: White Russian
Job: Metaphysics, camping	Exercise: My brain

Who do you most look like?
Audrey Hepburn

Beach or mountains?
Mountains, duh

What's on your bucket list?
Learn to ride a Harley

Margaret Thatcher

<u>Abstract:</u> Excerpt from *British Peerages, Volume IV*: Baroness Thatcher, LG, OM, DStJ, PC, FRS, HonFRSC; Education: Somerville College, Oxford. Major: Emasculation. Currently: Owner of lobbying firm with goal of becoming Prime Minister's wife and creating popular political ideology known as Thatcherism.

BLITZ CHICK / BATTLE OF BRITAIN

Our story...

One afternoon, as the sun is dipping under the horizon and the Home Guard has taken up defensive positions near 10 Downing Street, a man glances at his phone and sees that a woman has sent him a "like" on Spitfires.com. Upon examination of her profile, he thinks, well, she doesn't seem to be a bunny boiler so I'll message her. After a few exchanges, she suggests they meet in person. He's a bit taken aback because he's not used to a woman taking the lead with a draft dodger but agrees to meet her anyway.

About an hour before they're supposed to meet he thinks to himself, why am I doing this? Can I text her and say my dog is throwing up on my new carpet? At the same moment, she's thinking, why did I suggest meeting? Good grief, there's a World War going on! And if I wear these WAAC boots, I'm going to be taller than him. But because they were both brought up to be polite, they reluctantly head to the destination point, a park where there are nearby bomb shelters in case of the inevitable Luftwaffe attack.

At the appointed time, they walk up to each other and hide their awkwardness behind phony smiles. They both lie and say they're excited to be going on this walk on such a fine day. Isn't it so much warmer than it usually is this time of year? I didn't even know this path had survived the last bombing raid! Do you come here often? How long have you lived in this area? Heard about Dunkirk? Where are you from?

As they walk down the muddy path along the river, she tells him she was born in Lincolnshire, was a cheerleader at Oxford and that she got into politics because she was determined to succeed in a man's world; that she's an art lover-bibliophile and has written legislation and is part-owner of a niche political consulting business; how she's passionate about supply side economics and low estate taxes and hiking and making bandages at the Red Cross HQ; and, how she taught her young sons how to bait a hook, drive a car, shoot a Sten Gun, tell the truth and prep for Parliamentary debates.

Just as they come to a fork in the path, they both think to themselves, I haven't once looked at my watch this whole time and no air raid sirens yet! By the time they come to the footbridge, they're laughing and having a grand ol' time. By the end of their walk, they're relaxed and enjoying each other's company. As they walk towards the parking lot past the Bofors 44mm anti-aircraft gun emplacement, he says to her, Louis, I think this is the beginning of a beautiful friendship (Casablanca). She turns to him with a big smile and says, I'm glad you didn't text to cancel because your dog was barfing all over your new carpet.

OK, that's the end of my silly story. Please reach out if you want to go on this walk with me or something else. BTW, I am tetanus immune thanks to Pfizer. My sincerest wishes to you in finding your true love and good luck during this crazy Blitz!! Mags

Gallery

NO ONE ROCKS A HAT BETTER

MEETING MY PEEPS.

OLE JIMMY GETTIN' JIGGY

Why do I have to do this?

Widowed

Kids: Twins – live on their own

Religion: Anglican

Race: British

Exercise: None of your damn business

Drink: Tea (Madame Chiang's Herbal)

Education: Oxford (where else?)

Athletic/fit: None of your business

Smoke: Indeed!

Job: Lobbyist

Currently reading: Exhequer's Estimate of VAT on Braided Textiles, *The Kitty Kelly Story*.

Most spontaneous thing I've done...

Answer this question.

I got in the most trouble for...

Placing a whoopee cushion under Neville Chamberlain's hassock

Bucket List

Make the quarterfinals at next year's ParcheesiFest! in Madrid.

Caesar Chavez

<u>Abstract:</u> From Indeed.com resume: "C-Suite executive who opens the line of communication between clients, customers, and businesses to get agricultural operations unionized. With more than 20 years of fieldwork in the public, private, and tomato picking sectors, Chavez has experience in management confrontation and team building. Demonstrated success in picket line synergies and plant shutdowns at Del Monte and General Foods, ultimately leading to his nomination for the 1971 Nobel Peace Prize. Holds a high school diploma from Bakersfield Tech and combines progressive politics with Roman Catholic symbolism. No justice, no peace, no strawberries!"

CC Rider / Bakersfield

Pequeña biografía!
HOLA senoritas!! *Encantada de conocerte y gracias por pasar por aquí!* I bet you don't see too many brown brothers on this site so guess what, it's *es tu dia de suerte!*

No, we don't all cut grass for a living. Indeed, a significant cohort of Latinx are bilingual and *si*, communicate with erudition and verve. Say it loud *soy en hombre* I'm proud! If you're game, then *vamos mujer!* Grab your sombrero and let's take a little trip south of the border. *Hi-ya ole!*

Un poco about ole CC Rider. I have jet black hair and my current biographers describe me as being "outwardly shy and unimposing." But what do those pointy-head *gringos* know?!

As with many former farm laborers, I have experienced severe back pain throughout my life. I am self-conscious about a lack of formal education and I am often uncomfortable interacting with affluent people. Hey, you're born in a squatters camp to 15-year-old parents and suddenly RFK is seeking your advice on labor law?! *Dáme un respiro!* Who can blame the Caleinete Kid? Probably the most astute thing said about me was that I "thrive on the power to help people." And that's why I'm here. I want to help you help me.

Because the fact is, I'm not just a leader of the dispossessed, the despised, the despairing. I also have hopes and dreams. *And Needs.* And not just for Mama's delish *tortas de tamales! Si,* I find myself on the road a lot so while I list Bakersfield as home base you're just as likely to find me in Delano or Yuma and sometimes when I'm feeling a bit nutty and need to get my batteries recharged, I crash with some pals in an orchard outside San Bernardino.

But there's also a serious side to the ole Chavista. I know about life, *muchasos* – the endless workshops at the Rockefeller Foundation, the tedious fundraisers in Beverly Hills - c'mon *mesero,* forget about the Zinfandel, get this *hombre* a cold *cervesa!* The rallies with aggrieved wokesters and upper-class suburbanites, the motorcades that stretch forever with no scheduling for smoke breaks - *aiii!* It's the usual story: Classically overworked senior executive on a G-6 in faraway airports and the so-called first-class hotels with third-generation Echelons they "claim" are Pelotons. *Gringo,* don't try to con the conman.

Sure, I've been on LatinAmericanCupid.com but there's a dreary sameness there. Those *senoritas* are just looking to cash out and Caesarino is not going to play their game.

Por el amor de Dios! I'm so tired of games! I see enough of them in the historic ethnic stratification of contemporary society and the longstanding - and might I add, exceedingly justified - reluctance of my brothers and sisters to engage with law enforcement officials of any stripe. *No mas,* ladies! CC is in the *casa* for sure, but let's don't burn it down around us with your unthinking non-intersectional white adjacency!

Given my simplicity and sincerity, I would like to find a woman that looks past my brown skin and sees a real human being – one with, as noted above, hopes. *And Needs.* My life is not important – but yours is. That's because you like opera, the Sunday *Times* spread across a Knoll Platner coffee table surrounded by plates of bagels and lox and that Cactus Fruit Pico de Gallo that can only be provisioned at Baldacci's. You are at home in a Cartier gown as you are in burlap sack and you always can always be found in sensible boots at a workers' rally. You read Camus but don't really believe him and in any case consider him inferior to Vascancelos. You're ready to bring a little Latin loop-de-loop into you *libre est estadow, que pasa?* You feel me, mama?

I'm a Navy vet and yes, a U.S. citizen so let's get that little elephant out of the room.

/

So toma mi mano, leave the Anglo world behind and come with me south of the border. There's more to this world than the upper 48. I'll take you where the sun never sets and where the *frijolies* grow in trees. Caesar beckons, and if you know a good masseuse, that's a bonus.

Gallery

ME AND MY MAIN HOMBRE, RFK

IF IT'S TUESDAY, THIS MUST BE FRESNO...SIGH

IT'S ALL ABOUT JUSTICE. *AND NEEDS.*

Aiiii!
Separated
Five kids: sometimes live at home
Want kids? Si!
Religion: Roman Catholic
Drink: Grupo Medelo
Job: Boycott consultant

Education: Not really
Athletic/fit: A few extra tacos

Smoke: *Bueno!*
Race: Don't pigeonhole me!
Exercise: Tomato harvesting

Can't leave home without this
Leaflets

If loving this is wrong, then I don't want to be right:
Shutting down the Whole Foods distribution center in Long Beach

Favorite Tool
Cusinart filled with margaritas!

Eleanor Roosevelt "Grools"
Henry David Thoreau

Well. Walden Hunkster. How *do* you __do__? I couldn't help but stare at your profile – you rugged he-man. It's your Hyde Park Puma here and may I say I am truly taken by your gusto. My Christian name is Elly and while I don't know what a Jake Chillenthal is, I do know a Hunkster when I see one and you are one and I see you. You must simply tell me about this transcendental hobby of yours. Sounds so masculine – a clash of the dualities as such? I go for the blood moon in any cycle. Tell me all about your wood chopping antics.

Yo Elly, what be shakin' in your hogwarts? All be chillax at the pond. I really dug your profile. Out of sight, finchkins. Sounds like your old man was a total noam chomsky. Yeah, the Emersonian dealio I'm on right now – major league recommend it for your flow. My real name is Hank, or Hanka the lanka and you know it - when I get my choppin' on its fabiola time.

Tell me, do you have any photographs of you chopping wood? And did you ever work in a factory? Or have a friend who does?

Yeah, spent a spell in the old man's graphite enterprise – rog, you read that right – I worked in a pencil factory (wink). Indubiously. I know my way around heavy-duty machinery like a mule with peepers. I also do a little bit of trailblazin' donchaknow. You saw my crib – it's dope. You seem to be beastin' an inner yearning. I feel you, jubby. Any plans for the weekend?

The usual booge – a meeting at the UN, take in a Broadway show – Guys and Dolls is all the rage. I simply would love to have you on one of my radio broadcasts from that splendid wrap-around porch of yours. Do tell me about the factory! I bet it gets hot in there and everyone foregoes undershirts. Do you lift large tongs of steel and coke whilst the furnace ovens belch fire, the sweat dripping off your face and forearms and all over your leather trousers? I bet you you're surrounded by cowokers all as muscular as you.

Natch, just as you describe. The sweet toil of labor – it contributes to the subliminal serenity that is my frame of reference. I'm thinking you might like a pause from the cause – that Hyde Park scene with all the waco-fake-o. Groady. Whyncha take a trip up the Old Post Road and pay the Lanka a swing by? Past Falls River you take a left at the third Stuckey's and follow that footpath 14 furlongs, turn right at the mosque and swag-git until you see a sign that says, Lanka's Crib. It's carved into a 250 year old oak. And what's a radio?

CHAPTER 5

Playas, Posers, and Bunny Boilers in the 3ʳᵈ Millennium A.D.

2000 to Tomorrow
Mike Ditka
Cher
Biggie Smalls
Kim Jong-un
Rihanna

Mike Ditka

<u>Abstract</u>: From *NFL Legends*: "Born Michael Dyczko in Carnegie, PA. An American former football player, coach and television commentator, Ditka is a member of both the College (1986) and the Pro (1988) Football Halls of Fame. He was an NFL champion with the 1963 Bears and is a three-time Super Bowl champion, playing on the Cowboys Super Bowl VI team as well as winning one as an assistant coach for the Cowboys in Super Bowl XII and coaching the Bears to victory in Super Bowl XX. He is one of only two men to win an NFL title as a player, an assistant coach, and a head coach. Currently: Seeking interested franchisees for Ditka Steakhouse opportunities in the Buffalo/Erie metropolitan area."

Iron Mike / Chi

Yeah, me

Lemme tell you something, chickee birds, when you've been in as many locker-rooms as Iron Mike you know damn fast there are two types of men in this world: Mamas boys and winners. Now don't get me wrong here - I love my Ma – she's a tough old hen and she makes the best kielbasa this side of Toledo. But some young fellas never leave Mama behind. They never make it to the sandlot between the railroad tracks and the union hall where you prove yourself against other winners and if you get hurt you rub some dirt on it and pull up your breeches and fight on, dammit.

Why is Coach on this pansy site? I'll tell you why because I don't have no secrets from nobody. You stack a 4/3 defense in work and life and you make no apologies. Now listen up! My secretary Madge had it up on her computer screen one day as I was walking by to the film room. All these mugshots were on the screen and I said what is this, a Mamas boy convention? She said no, it's a dating service and since I broke up with Rocko I'm looking for true love again. Then she used what she calls her "scroll" function and showed me a few pansyass biographies or whatever the hell they're called. Freakin' wimps, every one of them. Madge, I says, look at these Mamas boys - leaning against their hot rods or holding up puny fish they caught. There's even a few punks who have photos of themselves sitting outside at a tiny table at some joint in Paris or Philly, holding a pansy tea cup and looking off into the distance like they forget where the hell they are. What the hell, I says to Madge, these are all Mamas boys, no winners need apply.

Since the well has been a bit dry for ole Coach lately I told Madge to throw me a bone and use her secretarial skills to make me a biography of myself and I dictated to her just what you are reading here on your application or whatever the hell it's called. Iron Mike doesn't have time to learn all this b.s. about radiowave electronics. The interweb don't respond to blitzes or cover 3.

But now I'm here and you little ladies have a real choice from all these tea drinking pinkie lifting weakasses on this site.

Name is Mike, Ma calls me Mike, you can call me Iron Mike. I don't believe in hiding behind all these wimpy screen names like Hunkster or DillyDeeBoy. Players call me Coach just like everyone else in the country. I'm a straight-no-chaser kind of guy and you better be too or you can just lick your finger and turn the page on your freakin' Apple thing.

You know where you'll find me? I'll tell you – in the fight. Where coaches coach and players play. Where there's pain and glory and fight. Where your strong side linebacker is always gonna save your ass and where there's no need for some candydancer weak safety or these whining Mamas boy cornerbacks with their fancy socks hopping around like ballerinas.

Now, a little about me. I am a former football player and then a football coach and now I'm on the television where I second guess a lot of football players and coaches. My buddies on the television set do the same thing. And ladies, we are never wrong. The only part of Iron Mike that isn't iron are my brass balls. Yeah, I said it. Deal with it.

I make my bones on a few steakhouses where winners come to put on the nosebag and fill their pie holes and its real beef, not this free range garbage. Those kinds of cows are pansies. I smoke cigars and drink whiskey and if you have a problem with that go find yourself some dandy boy sipping weakass tea on a street full of gypsies. But there's not all iron in Iron Mike. I kinda got a soft side – like when I play high stakes poker and or when I keep a sly lookout for franchise opportunities. And I love a good kielbasa.

So here's what coach has to say – leave the Mamas boys behind and if you're a pistol and a good looker take a shot on ole Iron Mike. Life is like a football game – yeah, sometimes you find yourself backed up in the red zone and that's when you're gonna want a guy like me, the guy who can scheme the 4/3 in your life and stop the fullback draw at the point of attack. Join the blitz with ole Mikey and I guarantee you'll control the line of scrimmage.

Gallery

CALMLY EXPLAINING THE 4/3 DEFENSE

BRASS BALLS. DEAL WITH IT.

<small>ONE OF MY JOINTS; FRANCHISEES WELCOME</small>

More about IronMike

Divorced

Kids: 4 – grownups.

Want kids? Hell no

Religion: 4/3

Drink: Jack

Job: Badass

Education: General studies

Athletic/fit: Gimme a break

Smoke: Stogies

Race: What the frick does this mean?

Exercise: Only when Iron Mike wants to

Currently reading: Yeah

Songs I like to sing in the shower
Man in the Mirror by Michael Jackson

Who do you most look like?
Me. Who the hell else?

Can't leave home without this
Four cigars, pocket flask, and make-up kit.

Things about me that surprise people
Absolutely freakin' nothing.

Cher

Abstract: From *Wikipedia*: "An American singer, actress and television personality. Commonly referred to by the media as the 'Goddess of Pop' she has been described as embodying female autonomy in a male-dominated industry. Cher is known for her distinctive contralto singing voice and for having worked in numerous areas of entertainment, perhaps best known as a solo artist with the *US Billboard/Hot 100* number-one singles `Gypsys, Tramps and Thieves,' and 'Dark Lady.' Her iconic anthem, `Half Breed', established her as a worldwide champion for indigenous peoples; she is also known for her work with endangered species. Currently: Runs Diversity, Equity and Inclusion seminars focused on Native American culture; corporate discounts available."

HALF BREED / EVERYWHERE

OMG!!

It's a Long & Exasperating Story, But My Wish 4 All Of Us Is a Better Tomorrow,2 Help Someone Have a Better Day, You Can Give a Smile With Ur Eyes, Or Say "Hey, Next Yrs Gonna Be Better." Im So Sorry Life Is Scary / darling ,Tried 2 Write Something 2Lift Ur Spirits, Like Kaavan's Story, 2Bring Smile & Bit Of Happiness,& Hope . We Are Friends, We Come & Go, We Laugh,Get Pissed, ,,.I Can't See You But I Feel You..As You Are,… Its Like Ur essence. You're Not Alone / / … PLEASE PROTECT YOURSELF…I Want You To Be Here,So We Can Enjoy Life Together. I

Want You To See & Hear What I'm creating.I Want You To Be Here To Enjoy Your Lives,So We Can Laugh & Be Silly & Serious Together.We Are Family,& Cant Lose!!!!

I am a child of spontaneity and a grandmother of essence….YOU, my 3.871M Twitter peeps SAY THAT! THANK YOU!! I truly live for YOU not me and Kaavan!! My KAAVAN!!! THE Asian elephant Shackled in Shed MOST OF HIS LIFE. When Kaavan meeting w/Girlfriend Lucy in Islamabad HAPPY and now Lucy Stands Alone in Snow. Heart Breaks 4 her.She Belongs in Cambodia With Kaavan.Would you tie ur Dog alone Out in the Snow 4 days on end???

Animal rights are HUMAN RIGHTS!!!!

BTW /why am I here?! IN this PLACE IN my life…// Why do I PLACE my soul so vulnerable and bold in front of you creepy leering macho MEN… as my song goes when Neil DIAMOND joined me on stage that night at Caesars---- 'My life since then has been from man to man, But I can't run away from what I am';/ Why are all of you so deceitful and shallow AND narcissistic? DO you ever show glimpses of HUMANity??!!! If you're still reading this and haven't been shamed onto the next profile, then maybe you have the cahones that I've NEVER FOUND. Now, a little about me:

I'm a Half-Breed for THE WHOLE takes her to the metaphorical rez outside an imaginary town. Yes, a Half Breed…How I LOVE and HATE the word. People were against me since the DAY I WAS BORN!!//

STanD and & B Counted or Sit & B Nothing. Don't Litter,Chew Gum,Walk Past Homeless PPL w/out Smile.DOESNT MATTER in 5 yrs IT DOESNT MATTER THERE'S ONLY LOVE&FEAR / Don't know What Deal is with"Publishers Clearing House",Seems Legit . Makes Me So Happy to See Looks on Ppl's faces when They've just Been Told they'll Get 4 Rest of Their Life,& Can Choose another person to collect 5K a Month.They look like They Really Need it

Enough about me. But you should also know I'm in emotional recovery from two serious LTRs, both with prominent men who were DEEPLY flawed and knew it and told me and I DIDN'T listen. Perhaps it was their flaws and defects that so attracted me. I wanted to fix them and they ended up fixing me and so I LEFT THEM! KAAVAN!!! Both were entertainers – one a wisecracking, buoyant, happy-go-lucky deeply flawed person. The other a morose poet of hillbilly verse and also a deeply flawed person. With one I played the magical marionette – a perfect id to a playful ego. To the other I played the perfect muse, the angel with the harp to the hick with a country shtick.

And speaking of muses, I have one…My muse speaks of wood smoke campfires at dusk, the jangle of old pots holding buffalo stew…. My father married a pure Cherokee and my mother's people were ashamed of me, The Indians said that I was white by law, The White Man always called me Indian Squaw…We never settled, went from town to town…When you're NOT WELCOME you don't hang around, The other children always laughed at me, 'Give her a feather, she's a Cherokee' Half-breed, that's all I ever heard Half-breed, how I learned to hate the word, Half-breed, she's no good they warned ..MORE - of the cries of coyotes across the Platte River and the bird whistle of a brave in the bush… It's the cry, mournful and soulful, of the HEART AND LOVE in us all, even the Half Breed….. I can hear it. Can you? I SINCERELY doubt IT!!!?!?

Islamabad, Myanmar, England, Phnom Penh, Hamburg England….Makes me having horrendous Jet lag.Cant stay awake during day,& sleep in the night…Can't Think Clearly.Shouldn't text till I get decent nights Sleep. ….Go Between PISSED OFF & TEARS When I Tweet . I Do My Best,But Dyslexia's Like Betsy DeVos..A BITCH /

OH, this girl has seen it all. I've written best sellers - Forever Fit, which teaches us womyn healthy lifestyle absent grains and carbs and First Time, a delightful journey about my incredible life. I'm known as the Queen of Camp, the Goddess of Pop, and some call me "the best damn thing on

Twitter!" Why there's even talk at DreamWorks about a bio pic, People ask, will the "Strong Enough" singer take the lead role for herself?" I haven't DECIDED!!!///.

You know I almost NEVER DELETE MY TWTS,But Sometimes No Matter how you Feel,Better to keep it to yourself.Doesn't Make any Difference what Others Do,Or Say.There are lines you can't Cross. I'm Not Important / Bt KAAVAN is Alwys....I know, with our climate we should not even have ZOOS?!! Nobody goes half the year. And taxpayers pay for it- the zoo does not generate enough revenue from tickets/sales/donations to run. They receive taxpayer funded grants . KAAVAN is expensive to care for so we MUST ALL HELP OUT!!! AHHHHH, three phones last night & None Of Them Worked.

 Like I told Amanapour on Raydio.., "I kept thinking of myself as a bumper car, and I thought 'If I hit the wall, I'll come back and I'll go another direction.'"

"I kept thinking of myself / bumper car...Did I Tweet About Lucy in Islambd Alone in the Snow & Bua Noi / in Shri Lanka In Fkng Shopping mall, they call a Zoo ...Did I Ask You to help me,Like You Asked Me To #FreeKaavan ,or did I Just Dream It They're Both Prisoners .Dream About them Suffering Most Nights

You know... I Wld like UR Help Locating Mistreated Animals../ The Wild / Good People Of Bangkok I Know You Will Understand & Help Me Stop The Torturing Of Innocent Animals. It Is a Sin.Please Help Me Bring Peace to these Animals. &Free Them From Pata Zoo...Shopping Mall Inshallah.

btw / A holiday special for you: @scentbeauty offering 50 SIGNED bottles of Cher Eau de Couture on their website right now! https://scentbeauty. com/products/cher-eau-de-couture-holiday-signed-bottle

I'm not like other girls on this site – I'm looking for a soul brother and a soul father, not soulmate. Preferably in a non-entertainment field - finance, medicine, or high-end retail would be ideal. KAVAANN!!!!Someone to walk the trail of tears. Someone who lives and breathes the champagne of unrequited Mother spirit in all things great and good. And you should live within two miles of Sunset near Brentwood or on the Upper West Side, preferably below the Starbucks on 72nd.

Namaste Buanoi's Been In Solitary Long Enough.Torturing ANIMALS 2 Amuse Mindless Shoppers Is a Sin.Hell Finally Rains Down On Those Who Commit This CRIME. LOCK UP MUST COME 2 AN END 4 BUANOI & OTHER #freeBuanoi #FreeTheWild #FreeThemAll Help Me, Free them

I'm just a poor Armenian girl who made it bigger than anyone has a right to make it. My own unbelievable life is not important to tell you now. When we meet, I can tell you and I know you will be impressed. The infinite beckons. Can you help me find it? I DOUBT IT!!!

Gallery

MY COUNTRY PHASE. THAT JERK.

IF U GOT IT SHOW IT!

KAAVAN!!!!!

My INCREDIBLE LIFE!

Divorced

Kids: 2

Want kids? In this world???!!!

Religion: Pisces / Moon Rising

Drink: The moon

Job: Twitter

Currently reading: Instagram

Education: Hollywood

Athletic/fit: ALWAYS!!!

Smoke: Newports. And defile my temple?!

Race: Animal Kingdom

Exercise: Bikram Choudhury is a bestie.

Most spontaneous thing I've done

Write a No. 1 country music hit.

Something I'm legitimately bad at:

I don't know

Things about me that surprise people

Bowled a 300 at Astro Lanes in Riverside, California

Biggie Smalls

<u>Abstract</u>: From *BustaMove.com*: "Born Christopher George Latore Wallace in New York in 1972, he is best known by his stage names: the Notorious B.I.G., Biggie Smalls, or simply Biggie. An American rapper and song-writer rooted in the New York rap scene and 'gangsta' traditions, Mr. Wallace is identified by a distinctive laidback lyrical delivery that offsets his lyrics' often grim content. His debut album *Ready to Die* (1994) was met with widespread critical acclaim, making him the central figure in East Coast hip hop and restoring New York's visibility at a time when the West Coast hip hop scene was dominating the genre. His music is semi-autobiographical, highlighting his own hardships and criminality but also debauchery and the celebration of parole violations. Currently: Engaged in good-natured feud with Tupac."

BIGGIE

IMO mf wordz

What's up yaw? Funk yo shizzle – Biggie beze in the datin' crib and bustin' some madz rimes for all the hos out dere lookinz' to ridez it and drivez it, you feel me? Chekkkit - Ize be the baddest mofo y'all ladies evah seen. With Biggie you be runnin' with the big dawgs. Ize not trying to scare ya'll off, jes keeping it reals. For *reals*. Ize be ons 'dis app cuz it be time 'fo Biggie to gits a ho that unnderstan' a conflicted playa. I allus be truff'ful, dat's why I gotz to bring it hard and tellz ya dere be two Biggies and I be wrasslin' wit 'dem all 'de time.

In retrospect, the fundamental discord emanates from a childhood of love, abundance and yet familial contradiction. Poppy was a noted Elizabethan linguist and poet. Mamam was a Professor of Inorganic Chemistry at Yale. Hence, me'ze childhood be all funked up. The old man applied sub-textual pressure to my artistic chromosomes with constant inculcation – some say indoctrination - of Browning and Milton recordings. Mama, in a non-traditional matriarchal role, spirited me from my cello lessons to her campus lab and her ground-breaking experiments in organometallic compounds. This parallel adolescent conjunctive was consonant with my own rather sizeable intellectual capacity but the materfamilias created a tortured duality in which, in the words of Eliot, the center would not hold.

Conflated well into my teen years at Greenwich Country Day School and coming under increasing pressure from my chess club posse on the village's mean streets, I unsteadily followed a modern Mosaic rite of passage and concluded I should follow my patriarchal super ego and foreswear the periodic table.

'Sho's nuff, somz' whack jobs soon be sayin' I beze 'de avatar of a new cultural expressionism - their words, of course. I had developed a voice, an almost mystical reverberation of centuries old groanings of a people unknown but strangely persistent in my conversations with my sub-conscious. Perhaps it was my skin color. Soon I was "bustin," as the nomenclature would have it, these "rimes," becoming a pied piper of modal verse coupled with a Caribbean beat that bespoke the tragedy of the ghettos in northeast Westport. Indeed, while I found it slightly liberating, the *Times* insisted I was "jammin with a verve that be crystallizing the struggles of a new generational cohort of angry, marginalized youth in the better zip codes." I was humbled. For you see, I was just following my muse.

Throughout this torment, I lost me, Christopher George Latore Wallace. I stopped my Pilates, began carbo loading and soon became the artist known as "Biggie Smalls," an identity that fawning critics called "a straight up homey." Sure, an entertainer with two Platinum records and 48-city concert tours, a lovely crew of jacked up and whacked out peeps living in the de moment, big ass crib in South Beach and seven vintage pre-war English automobiles.

But who was Ize? I dint' know. Psychologists were consulted in vain. None could fathom the dichotomized childhood fusion of 19th Century verse *vis a vis* barium stannate (BaSnO3). Oh, the odyssey of finding oneself! At one point, I didn't know where Mr. Christopher Wallace left off and Biggie Smalls began. *Even my stage name showed the duality of my inner conflict.*

I means, I was jackin' it, man. Getting' my thang onz! My posse be all! And then, as in all redemptive psychological invalidations, it hit me one afternoon during a driveby hit on the Darien Crips. Me crew beze' my life. Biggie be puttin' he bros before he hos and at some juncture, I found I had no mo hos no mo. So heres' I be. Lookin' 'fo 'dat special ho.

What do I seek? A Renaissance femme. You have an Art History degree from Smith but you were also captain of the women's swim team. You work at Goldman Sachs on the derivatives desk and like window shopping at Tiffany's and you wish Schrafts on 47th and Madison was still around for some of their yummy pecan pie. You have a certain Antifa assertiveness but you're never far from your needlepoint basket. You can be found in tartan skirts at knee level with black wool tights and sensible shoes. And you like Hennessy straight up.

At the same time, ya' booty gotz to be down with the Biggie life. You down with loadin' a Glock, able to ride horses, into the klub scene, and likes I be sayin', you best be into vintage pre-war English automobiles. And I meanz' the First War, mamma. You feels me? Someone who is at home in Compton as in Calabasas, Linkin' Park and Evanston, SoHo to 187th Street, and I mean the West Side, baby. And if you can sing backup, 'dat beeze' a bonus.

Maybe you're perusing this modest missive and you're reflecting, "'dat Biggie be speakin' to a partz of me. I too have lived the adolescent duality and the dichotomized fission of Muse vs. Carbon. He be touching my inner byotch and beze a talisman to my inner ho."

Make no mistake girlies, Biggie lead a life of danger – my rise in the arts has set loose de 'foces of disharmony in the 'hood called Life. Allus I ask if you want get jiggy with Biggie is that you takes my hand and feel 'de gold and 'de jewels that is my materialist reward for revealing the struggles I've borne. Walk down the dark alleys of introspection with Biggie and get down with you baddest self. Biggie be callin', Biggie be waitin', Biggie Biggie Biggie. In the affairs of the heart, Biggie never be Smalls.

Gallery

..BEZE SIGNIN' MY NAME YAW   HAPPY TIMES AS THE KING OF RAP!

FAME...ALAS   ALLUS 'BOUTS DE BENJAMINS

Meze

Separated   Education: Greenwich Country Day
Kids: 5 (I think)   Athletic/fit: Check my name, yo
Want kids? Dunno - prolly
Religion: Rimes   Smoke: rock, schwag, smack
Drink: Colt 40s   Race: Bed-Stuy Chieftains
Job: Poet 'o 'de projects,
vintage automobiles   Exercise: What dat?

Currently reading: Anything Agatha Christie

Thing about me that surprise people...
Play cello

One thing I would like to see most in the world
The sun rising on the total annihilation of the Darien 7th Street Crew

Favorite Foods
All

Bucket List
Win a Nobel Prize for Literature; float with the dolphins.

Cher "Triple Hearts" Dylan Thomas

WHO RU with UR DRUID Bobolinks?!?! I love your speak-writing. It reminds me of my first husband who had so many issues, speaking being one of them. I am SOOO like you – the ENGLISH language is dead! People say NOTHING anymore. That's what I tell my 3.71M Twitter followers. Language should be music and the other way around. Don't you think>!>!>! I had such a good time trying to understand your profile! Is DyllyDee U or your fake U?!?!

Skeek mumbly peg! What a fairies tale you spin with rosemary and Camelot crimson! I just rambledly through the sonnet of your life. Me speaks for the world in admiring your pachyderm obsession and meekins says animal rights are human rights as sure as a Bobolink's bobby!!! My dreaming heart unites with yours in shared rilly heartbeats for our kingdom's biggest and finest going beneath the Melodious Moon. You mentioned having a large manse on the Upper East Side. Pray tell what cross streets on the tiara of lights of that Manhattan fantasia?

LA BELLA LUNA!!! HOW did you KNOW!!?? Moonstruck was my fave movie to do of ALLLLL TIME!!!,. an epic $80.6 M at the box office five times gross over production cost. Ah, I remember it all …The starshine of romance and bestitiest best Nickie Cage a tender man though not without deep emotional flaws as with EVERY MAN I MEET!! SO many ISSUES! You sweet note made my heart ring so that I tweeted it to my 3.71M followers!! SO blissful – like when Kaavan was freed from that shopping mall in Dhaka in stupid Bangladesh and airlifted on a C-130 to THAILAND!!! You are SOOO CREATIVE. We need to collaborate on poems and music and songs….I have done that TWICE w/flawed muses!!!! WHAT do you talk about when you meet a druid?!?!!?

Randy wandies and keely kobs! Perhaps we can meet at your place and discuss this whole druid deal further. Me purse be holy but light – mightn't you spare doubloons for the steamship fare?

Kim Jong-un

<u>Abstract</u>: From the *CIA World Book 2021*: "Kim...was born 1982, 1983, or 1984...is an erratic but happy-go-lucky politician serving as Supreme Leader of North Korea since 2011. He is the second child of Kim Jong-il and the grandson of the nation's founder, Kim Il-sung. The youngest Kim is known for promoting the policy of *byungjin*, referring to the simultaneous development of both the economy and the country's nuclear weapons program. In 2014, a UNHRC report suggested that Kim could be put on trial for crimes against humanity but he laughs that off as a 'little misunderstanding.' Currently: Owner of the world's largest fleet of jet skis and host of the annual "Kimmer 007 RaceFest!" in the South China Sea.

KIMMER 007 / PYONGYANG

Press Release, Democratic People's Republic of Korea
"The light of thought is getting more and more dazzling in the headwind and against the current. Gazing at today's horizons, the shifting situation is intertwined with world-encountering changes unseen in a century and the trend of openness and accommodation is rolling forward. The global peoples turn their attention to North Korea seeking wisdom and solutions in this special historical period of new crossroads of open cooperation and economic success in an inclusive and win-win direction."

NANG!!! How's that for an intro to your newest best friend?! *Annyeonghaseyo* to all you Kimmy Kats! Still with me?! *Dangsin-eun ihaehab-Nang!! Nang?!*

It's your Kimmer here, everyone's pal! A friendly easygoing guy like the ones you see at your kid's rec soccer practice or in the herb aisle at the Whole Foods. But guess what!? It's the same guy whose day job happens to be running a seven-decade old empire that is a slice of heaven on earth, complete with upscale shops, fine dining and off-season beach resort packages that start as low as $450 *wons*, 5 days/4 nights, meals included! Everybody Wang Chung tonight!

It's a typical story – crazy busy dictator ruling a rogue nation and putting up with all the headaches – the whining peasants, the mad dog foreigners, the paperwork, those nail-biter missile launches. But trust me, everything's *nang.*

And your life, my Flower? Like mine? A triumph of will over hopelessness and disarray? Of course. That's what's makes this app so *keun* – it introduces you to me and our shared victories over all the calamities the world has thrown at us. Speaking of which, hasn't this virus been some deep *kimchi*!?

Now, here's my truth. I am a huge NBA fan – rockin' those Bulls and Lakers like white on rice! In fact, one of my close personal friends is Dennis Rodman, he of six – count 'em – NBA Championship Rings! But I have pals outside the hardwood. Why, check out this endorsement from President Trump: "I learned he was a talented man. I also learned he loves his country very much. He has a great personality and was very smart." Backatcha D-dawg!!

And while you might think I'm like every other guy on this platform, my lotus blossom, I'm not. Because like I said, very few have their own Army! But I don't ask for much, my little rice cake. Only that you have a great bod and like being driven in chauffeured Hummer limousine!! Just think of me as the guy next door who happens to own the whole town!! *Nang!!*

Gallery

SOME OF MY ARMY BUDDIES.

WTH! WHOSE THAT HANDSOME GUY ON THE RIGHT?!

NUKES FOR PEACE!!

Chong!
Separated
Kids (3) live with Mamasan

Education: Swiss *Ecole (speak French!)*
Athletic/fit: (ok, maybe a few *paundeu!*)

Want kids? Depends
Religion: My grandfather's
Drink: Seagrams' Raspberry
Wine Coolers
Job: Manager, NBA Fantasy League

Smoke: Bad for you

Race: DPRK!
Exercise: Power walks

Currently reading: Whitman's *Leaves of Grass*

If loving this is wrong, then I don't want to be right
A truck-launched Hwasong-14 Intercontinental Ballistic Missile

Fave place to hang out
Key Biscayne Ritz Carleton during the Jet Ski World Series

Beach or mountains?
Yes, my country has both.

Rihanna

Abstract: From *The Encyclopedia of Modern Composers (Volume VI)*: "Robyn Rihanna Fenty is a Barbadian singer, actress, fashion designer, and businesswoman. Born in Saint Michael to 16-year old parents, Ms. Fenty won early fame as a child voice prodigy and at 13 years of age was admitted to the Julliard School, taking her Doctorate in Chorale Orchestration. After appearances with the New York Philharmonic and Vienna Boys' Choir, she signed with DefJam label in 2005 and gained recognition with her first two studio albums, *Music of the Sun* and *A Girl Like Me*, both of which featured augmented Aeolian sixth chord variations. Her third album, *Good Girl Gone Bad* (2007), incorporated dance-pop and Heldentenor divertimento themes based on the 12-tone scale, establishing her status as a sex symbol in the music industry. She continued to mix contrapuntal pop *qua* mixolydian genres on following studio albums; *Talk That Talk* (2011) produced a string of chart-topping singles, including "Danube RastaMan" and "De higher de monkey climb de more he do show he tail." Currently: She is collaborating with Drake, Jay-Z, and the London Chamber Orchestra.

RIRI / BRIDGETOWN

Pull-up-dat!

Deys call me the Black Madonna but 'dats just for intersectional marketing platform purposes. Ize really 'de Black Mozart. I means, you rock an awesome bod and a woke story and it all be cheese on bread. But no one ever talks RiRi and her lifelong study of 'de Viennese School – and me meanz 'de First Viennese School. 'Dat becuz I alwayz be into 'de Austrian beatz, mon.

Mize inspiration comes from the Ameedaus and Ludwig, but me throw in Hayden in a cats paw moment. Amee's *Rondo Alla Turca?* The freakin' pistarckle! Dat oboe solo inspired 'de third track of 'de *Bad Girl* cd, 'Dingo Dango,' and me gotz me *Kiss It* platinum from liftin' a clam from Lud's *Erioca*, second movement. He bozzi!

But I do dabbles – went second V-school at age 22 and 'den flammed with Schoenberg on de 12-tone. De is more in de mortar dan de pestle wit heze *Verkiarte Nacht,* tru dat. Schonie was the bruggaflog for meze *Anti* cd in 2016. Indeed, I sought to use a bass clarinet for the concerto in "Shut Up and Drive" but my production manager overruled me. He be jerk.

Now, the sip sip on this sister be well known id 'de islands and ebby-where. What the maybe is? Some bad mistakes but all chill now. Domestic violence, multimillion-dollar breach of fiduciary duty, and that Saudi bastard. I also like ink. Lots of ink. In fact, I have a facsimile of Richard Wagner's signature on my sternum.

Ize be lookin' for a conchey Joe from 'de Strasbourg School. Someone who does not hit women, has never been audited by the IRS, is not from the Middle East and has a Ph.D from Julliard. I be *Wiener Klassik* mon and if you be too I fly you to my home in Barbados. It's on my private island.

Gallery

CHEGGITT!

ENCORE, *BUDAPEST BASSO CONTINUO*

MEZE INK!

GRADUATION, JULLIARD

'de cellardoor
Separated
Kids: Proud auntie!
Want kids? Buzzilickum!
Religion: Rastafarian

Education: Barbados Elementary
Athletic/fit: Cheggit' me pix

Smoke: Gunja

Drink: Mauby drink   Race: Rastafarian
Job: Me bod   Exercise: da beatz, mon

Currently reading: NYSE Annual Report

If loving this is wrong, then I don't want to be right
My Gulfstream G650

Songs I like to sing in the shower
Overture to *The Marriage of Figaro*

Who do you most look like
Madonna

Things about me that surprise people
Own 'de two Papa John's franchises on St. Kitt's

Biggie Smalls "Jacks" Virginia Woolf

Yo Ginnie, Biggie up in your crib. Sheezy, what's a nice 'ho like you doin' on a funky app like 'dis?! You seems allus mixed up and Biggie peeps deuce time on 'yo read befo' unerstannin' it, which intrigues the hell out of this emasculated Greenwich homeboy. I divined from your penetrating biography a distinct searching, a missed grasp at reality - you be wrasslin' with 'de demons so extant to the conflicted artist. So what be up girl 'wit allus 'dat?!

Mr. Biggie. did you ever crank the engine on a Model T? Despite the total depravity of inanimate objects, the mechanistic release of explosive force is a metaphor for the ignition of a conscious soul.

You go, girl! Biggie be down with your razzlin' apothems. Indeed, in my inner sanctum as a tru' blood I be 'memberin' the William James monograph on 'de standalone subliminal as an amalgamation of experience 'wit causality. What be the clubs where you and 'yo posse chill?

Mr. Biggie. I have a room of my own. It is my refuge where I interiorize with a montage imprint of memory. I don't think this will work, Mr. Biggie. Your drybones contextualization is so Victorian.

Aw Gins, Biggie be beggin' – I gotz a gangsta love for you...

The Single in the Arena

"Hope in love springs eternal" observed the 18th-century poet Alexander Pope. Easy for him to say IMHO inasmuch as he was in an LTR with Lady Mary-Montagu, she of the Nottingham Peerage, LOL.

In just a brief hour we've swiped left through 23 action-packed centuries and 21 of their historic titans, truly an incalculable panorama of achievement and ardor; nay, a timeless vista of the unsearchable, mysterious search for companionship, for affection, for a maiden or a beau or even a 'pookie-pie,' however one is defined in the ageless lexicon of love. But now of course, all is perhaps less mysterious.

While happily married readers are now snuggling with self-congratulation *vis-à-vis* their station in life, a few Western scholars and 41 million dating app enthusiasts have no doubt found consolation - even hope - with the archeological and dark Web gems unearthed for display in this slender volume. While varied in nature and nuance from the jocular to the down-right jiggy, all coalesce to provide a melodic universality to the rhythms of the soul; in the incomparable words of RiRi, "'da beatz 'o 'de heart, big-up mon!"

Our profiles in courage, *for that is what they are*, demonstrate that the brave hearts chronicled here were not lost in modern victimization nor ancient self-pity because of their status as "unattached." Quite the contrary. In fact, these champions live up to the stirring words of Hyde Park Puma's

Uncle Teddy-Wampums, *aka* Theodore Roosevelt, in his epic 1910 speech at the Sorbonne in Paris, "The Single in the Arena":

> "It is not the critic who counts; not the happily betrothed who sneer at the dogged man or woman who despairs of receiving a few likes - and those from Nigerian bots - or who mocks the Premium upgrade TurboBoost that results in numerous views from certified creeps. No, the credit belongs to the Single who is in the Arena - who pays their app subscription fees, routinely checks their phone, updates their photos, who strives valiantly to find a connection in boring phone calls and stifling conversations at a noisy Starbucks or Chili's. The Single knows there is no effort without error and shortcomings and ridiculous emoji-laden texts. That's because these stalwarts are also the ones who know great enthusiasms; who at their best know the triumph of several promising dates and who at their worst, if he or she fails, at least fails while logging into their account thrice daily - so that their place shall never be with those cold and timid souls who never got on a dating app and thus live in a grey twilight that knows not victory nor defeat"

Powerful words and all true of course, natch. Our needy bachelors and bachelorettes have indeed achieved glorious triumphs and won historic acclaim for unsurpassable deeds. Even so, they strive for *something more.*

Always there is their quest for companionship – the relentless drive for an LTR, a relationship, or even just a situationship.

Always, always – there is the desire throughout the ages to Meet Someone New.

ABOUT THE AUTHOR

NELLIE / SANTA MONICA

About me!

Thanks for stopping by!! I know you have hundreds of guys to choose from on this app so you're fortunate to land here! And girls, it's bonus time because I have no problem talking about myself (☺) so here we go!

I am a fun-loving, modest, and highly acclaimed academic who always sees... wait for it...the glass three-quarters full! Bang!

Now, I know you're wondering "What does he like?" ...hmmm...I like holding puppies, sunset walks along the beach (any beach without rocks!), the smell of a double latte with a splash of non-fat milk, spelunking and travel – especially travel! I've been to six different states and hope to add to that number as soon as I can get a vaccination appointment 😷. I'm a bit of a gearhead – love to take apart old washing machines and leave them that way! Btw, fun fact: Did you know there is no "I" in team but there is a "me"!!

Enough about me. Let's talk about the perfecto girl I'm seeking – how about one with a heartbeat - ha! - told you I was funster (☺)! Ok, Nellie will go to serious mode-ski here: A down-to-earth super-smart and super-athletic and super-successful independent woman who loves and lives and most important, listens. A lot. A girl who is at home in jeans as she is in overalls… who adores editing tedious manuscripts but also has a fun side with her career in option derivatives trading…whose favorite places to visit are are Busch Gardens and Branson…who can laugh at funny things and also my humor!!

If this all strikes a match and lights a fire, then I'm only a ♥ away! If not, darn! I guess I'll have to go get another double latte!!

Gallery

ME AT THE GYM; I ONLY SMOKE
DURING WORKOUTS!

A MATCH DATE IN TAIPEI
OUR THIRD MEETUP!!

MY THREE MILITARY OFFICER SONS, ALREADY MORE SUCCESSFUL THAN DAD!

Sketch
Currently reading: eHarmony.com

If loving this is wrong, then I don't want to be right:
Finding a woman who hasn't read *Eat Pray Love*

Things about me that surprise people:
My bobblehead collection of characters from Dante's Inferno

If a documentary was made about my life it would be...
35 minutes long

These are on my Bucket List:
Fall in love, change someone's life for the better, swim with the dolphins, eschew cliches forever

Made in the USA
Middletown, DE
01 September 2021